SERPENT'S EGG

SERPENT'S EGG

SERPENT'S EGG

A FANTASY
by

R. A. LAFFERTY

MORRIGAN PUBLICATIONS
1987

SERPENT'S EGG

Published by
MORRIGAN PUBLICATIONS
84 IVY AVENUE
BATH, AVON, BA21AN

Cover design by Neil McCall

FIRST EDITION

TRADE EDITION ISBN 1 870338 10 3
SPECIAL EDITION ISBN 1 870338 15 4

Typeset and printed by
Bath Press Ltd, Lower Bristol Road, Bath, Avon

CONTENTS

CHAPTER ONE

THE THREE CORNERS OF THE WORLD

Therefore think of him as a serpent's egg . . .
And kill him in the shell.
                              Julius Caesar. Shakespeare

"The computers have taken up Astrology on their own," Lord
Randal's father had said one morning at breakfast. "Even the
Kangaroo is into Astrology now."

"How odd," Lord Randal's mother had answered. "That could
be quite dangerous. Computers do not distinguish between a
prediction and an instruction. They will try to make every one
of their predictions come true, even if they know it is silly. Do
not you yourself have doubts sometimes of our 'Floating
World'?"

"Those who have doubts of such things, Iris, may have the
Kangaroo to deal with. If they are important enough. But we
are border-line, not quite mega persons."

Well, why should this little scrap of breakfast conversation
by Lord Randal's parents have frozen the Lord with fear? He
surely wasn't a fearful boy. And why when he was frozen with
fear, should the same numbing fear have seized on his two close
associates? The other two had not even heard the scrap of conversation; but the other two always shared any emotion that one
of them shared.

These three had been raised together from their beginnings
until now when all three of them were between nine and ten
years old. The three were Lord Randal and Inneall and Axel.
They were so close, and they generated so much power from

1

their closeness, that Axel had once proposed that they adopt two lines from Swinburne for their motto:

'Where three men stand together
Are kingdoms less by three.'

"Oh, that won't work at all," Inneall had uttered. "We are no men at all. We are one girl and two boys."

"What I am worried about is what the Kings of those Kingdoms will do when they feel themselves threatened," Axel worried. "And some king or kings *have* felt themselves threatened already by us. Remember the 'Serpent's Egg' anxiety or premonition."

That had been another scrap of breakfast conversation by George Lynn-Randal and Iris Lynn-Randal the parents of Lord Randal.

"We are suspected of harboring a Serpent's Egg," George had said.

"Which one? Oh, which one of them?" Iris had questioned him. "I'll miss any of my children that is killed, but I'm afraid that I'll miss Lord Randal more than either of the other two. That is very unfair of me, isn't it? When?"

"If it comes, it always comes just before the tenth birthday. A Dolophonos has already been put on standby for our case. I see him lurking around the 'jungle'. But that is done in the case of almost any experiment that can go wrong. But the one who is the Serpent's Egg always has a premonition of it somehow. But it doesn't happen often, only about one in a million of the general population is ever adjudged to be a Serpent's Egg."

"I've heard that it is as high as one in a thousand in some of the special experiments, but we don't know whether ours is that special or not. I do wish we had some idea of what the experiment is to indicate."

"This experiment of which we are the 'parents' is to explore 'New ways of looking at the world, but not too cockeyed new' is the only leak I've been able to get hold of."

It had been Axel who had overheard that scrap of breakfast conversation, but all three of them had begun to shake and shiver at the same time, and their spirits have not stopped shaking yet. They did not completely understand it, but it scared them all the way through. And it puzzled them. They knew that all

2

the venomous and dangerous serpents are viviparous, live-born, and have no eggs in the popular sense of eggs. They knew that only the harmless and benevolent snakes lay eggs, and who would want to kill such pleasant creatures in the shell that they do not have?

"There is a fury behind all this," Inneall said, "and fury does not have to be rational."

Lord Randal was a human boy though conceived in a glass tube. Inneall was an Ambulatory Mime-Human Computer, entirely mechanical except for a light-minded polter who dwelt in her part of the time, a tenant that the 'parents' of the experiment didn't know about. Her grammatical gender was male. By all rational rules she was sexless. And yet she insisted that she was a girl, and her insisting made it so. Axel was a simian of the species called Axel's Ape, sometimes called the Smithy Apes, for in their wild state they possessed the talents for working metals. They were sometimes called the Golden Apes for their color was such, and they were sometimes called the Blue-Eyed Apes.

These three were raised together from birth as part of an ongoing experiment. For their own area they had two hectares or about five acres of contrived feral land. That was really a large allotment for land was not as easily come by as it had been in former times. The area was shared however with other experiments: experimental plants, insects, experimental mammals and marsupials, fat sloths and tapirs and bandicoots and hogs that fed on rotten wood and mould and mulch and fissured rocks. There were experimental worms that weighed more than a ton each and were edible, though as yet they had rather sickening after-effects. There were experimental fish growing large and fat on the nutrient-mud that formed in the streams and pools faster than they could devour it. There were fat fowl that could fly 'thus far and no farther', for the two hectare plot had a transparent cover over it. There were experimental bread-bushes and honey-cane, and fat-berry vines. It was a picturesque small area with three leaping water-falls, with cliffs and clefts, with an almost natural interlocking support system.

But The Three realized very early that it was not completely natural (they seemed to have innate ideas of what was natural and what was not). Those water-falls had an element in addition to their natural state (should it therefore be called supernatural?): there were transparent tubes, hardly to be seen, in the middle

3

of the tumbling water-falls, by which the water was conveyed up to the top of the falls again. These were the only water-falls that The Three had ever seen, but they knew that the tubes didn't belong in the natural order of things.

And the vines by which they swung from the alpha cliff to the beta cliff above the water, they were live vines with green leaves growing on them. And yet they had something non-live twined in with them, metallic wire, so that these particular vines could never break even though other vines of apparently the same sort could be cut and broken. This strengthening wire was not in the natural order of things, and The Three knew it. It was of the mechanical order, the order of things that Inneall was made out of. And the cover over their area, there was something questionable about that. It was Axel who proposed a challenge to that transparent cover when they were all six years old.

Lord Randal had invented the bow-and-arrow. But Axel could shoot the arrows farther and faster. And higher. And when he was six years old, Axel did what many persons have dreamed of doing: he made his mark on the sky. He dipped the heads of his arrows in mud, and he shot them up with uncanny accuracy and made mud marks on that transparent sky-cover which was twenty meters above them. He made about a hundred mud marks that conveyed a message in the written form of 'code Chaldee' that the three had independently reinvented. The message was "If there is anybody up above that sky, let him give us a sign." And the sign came at once, quick lightning and a water shower on the top side of the sky. The Three were pleased to see that their message was not washed away by the rain shower. There was someone else out there, someone more important than the overly-silent care-takers who sometimes came into the area to make major or minor adjustments, trying to look invisible when they came.

The Three had lived in the lightly-covered area since they were a week old. What? A machine might live there when no more than a week old. An Axel's Ape, for all that we know different, might have survived. But how could a human boy have lived in such circumstances? What would he eat?

Oh, he would eat experimental truffles for one thing. They grew right under the surface of the ground, and some of them burst through the surface. They had an odor that was stronger and more enticing than fresh milk. And they could be sucked in as easily as milk. Then there was experimental taro root, and experimental yams that could be eaten almost as soon, by the age of three months anyhow. And then Lord Randal was not an ordinary boy. He was a boy bred and vitro-ed to have an I.Q. clear off the scale. With all three of them, the scanners had chirped early and often the warning "Mega, Mega, Mega!" to signify that they were exceptional persons or mega persons. And these warnings were recorded and pondered in the proper places.

When they were all one year old, a door was opened for them from their area to the back door of the Lynn-Randal house. And The Three wandered in to explore. As they explored everything they could enter, they here began the second aspect of their lives.

All three of them could walk well in their own manner by this time. All of them could talk in their several codes and tongues. They had no trouble in understanding the talk of George Lynn-Randal and Iris Lynn-Randal. The Three were very intuitive in these things. Within a week they already knew what these two grown persons would say before they opened their mouths. And yet the things in the Lynn-Randal house were quite interesting.

There was the music, an unparalleled encounter. The Three instinctively found their way to what they wanted in a collection of a hundred thousand tapes. Well, the tapes they played nearly drove the two adult Lynn-Randals crazy even though these tapes were of these adults' own collecting. There was a difference when they were listened to by other-way ears. The music came on a little bit too strong when melded with the minds of the three young entities. These listening minds gave entirely different contexts to the music.

There were pictures in the Lynn-Randal house. The Three had seen their whole world for their whole lives as kaleidoscopes of unframed pictures. There was nothing else in the world except pictures. But these pictures in the house (there were about thirty thousand of them on the one hundred dial-a-picture arrangements, and they were changed every month) had a special character.

There were smells in the Lynn-Randal house, and the Lynn-Randal adults themselves seemed insufficiently aware of some of them. These also had their special character. There were no smells quite like them in the whole outdoors. Though they had

5

a rather cloying element, yet they had the attractions of novelty. And it is well to have smelled every smell possible at least a few times.

And there were the animated talking books in the Lynn-Randal house. Well 'books', in that world that had entered its post-literary age, were the 'third tracks' of 'two-track prowls', and only a few of the 'prowls' were issued with this third track. But the Lynn-Randals believed in the three-track system, and they got three-trackers whenever they were available.

The first track was the sound, and the second track was the visual, both of them always a little bit sketchy to save money and to stimulate the imagination. High winds and thunder were usually in the background of the sound, along with the screaming of frightened alligators and the rutting cries of giraffes. These things were always 'good noise' even for sedate indoor scenes. The voices usually had the 'all-people throatiness' that had become the consensus voice of the media, now that it had been admitted that everyone was an ethnic and that there were no regular people left. Well, the last of the old supreme people had all been murdered on the charge (false) that they were unfeeling.

The pictures on the visual track were sketchy, sometimes film shots of real things, but mostly they were cartoons. Even the cartoon characters were fully drawn in only one frame out of every one hundred, and they were more perceived in subliminal than in clear conscious vision. This also was a great stimulus to the imagination. But every character in a prowl (sometimes the things were called 'antics' or 'romps' or 'trips' or 'experiences' or 'jaunts' as well as 'prowls') had its own bright and shining color, carried through from the drawn cartoon figures to the ninety-nine frames of rapidly-moving geometric forms. There was a lot of movement in those forms, and a lot of fragmented geometry.

In experiencing these prowls, The Three quickly discovered their own signature colors and geometries. Axel's was the golden pentagon with five arms at his five angles. Lord Randal was an orange square. And Inneall was a lavender-purple triangle. Whenever these colors and shapes turned up in the prowls, The Three could always identify themselves with the characters of those colors and shapes. And their identifications were always apt. The colored geometries taking the places of pictures of persons, besides saving money in the cartooning, were also a sort

6

of abstracting or psychologing of the characters, of finding their hidden essences.

The third track, whenever it was present in a prowl, was the printed word. At first meeting, each of The Three made an exciting and bizarre interpretation of the printing, but it was not the correct interpretation in any of the cases. Then they were told that it was not guesswork or whimsey as to what the printing meant. There were regular rules for interpreting it, and it was known as reading.

Axel was the first of The Three to learn to read. The week after they had all learned to understand human talk, Iris Lynn-Randal (the mother of Lord Randal) had read some of the printed prowls to each of them while following the text with her finger with the child gazing at it. Axel caught on immediately, and the other two did not. So she carried it through with Axel first. And in one week, Axel could read the printed prowls easily. It took the other two a month to master it.

"How odd," Iris said, "that the Ape should be the most intelligent of our three children. It is really impossible that he should have learned so quickly and well, and yet he has done so."

"We cannot say that one of our—ah—'children' as you call them—'experimental entities' is the right name for them—is more intelligent than the others," George Lynn-Randal stated, "since all three of them are designed to be so intelligent that they are clear off the scale. Above all, we must not forget that they *are* experimental entities. To become emotionally involved or sentimentally attached with them might destroy the validity of the experiment. In any case, it would be unwise for you. Twice before, you have suffered attacks of sentiment, and with disastrous results."

"Oh, George, I really believe that the results of my sentimentalities were more comic than disastrous," Iris spoke with that irritating grin of hers.

"Remember, Iris, that the majority of experiments will fail in the nature of things," George argued. "Be always ready to brush the ashes of this experiment off your hands if it fails."

"Nay, I'll pour the ashes of it over my head, and I'll wail and make mourn if it fails," Iris smirked. Oh, that Iris did have an irritating grin on her!

* * * *

"Just who *are* we three?" Inneall the little-girl computer asked Iris one day.

"You are The Three, always capitalized, to yourselves. The rest of the world will call you whatever it wishes."

"And will we always be just The Three?" Inneall pursued it.

"Probably you will combine with the children of other experiments when you are older. That's the way it was done when it was done that other disastrous time. Probably then you will become The Nine or The Twelve."

"Oh, that's all right then. That will show progress."

*   *   *   *

The bookish prowls were stylized and not really very good. They were supposed to be all sound and color and action, according to their advertising. But the real action, like the detailed drawings, happened in only about one frame out of a hundred. But there was never anything to take the place of the non-existent action. Some of the prowls were worse than others, and at the bottom of them all were the products of the 'Jackdaw Two-and-Three Track Press'. Jackdaw produced the 'Bongo and his Beepers' series, the 'Cut-Throats of Coke-Town' series, and the 'Fast-Action Eadie and Eddie' series. All of these had shovelings of noise and motion and color. All of them produced gnawing and garish blue moods, the same thing that tedium produces. All of these were for small children, for teenagers, and for adults alike. These were sometimes criticized, but mostly by persons of standards derived from an earlier age, from the pre-postliterate age. But the new ears of the new people could not recognize such things as satire or irony or rime. But, as the great contemporary philosopher Jasper Junkins (a pseudonym) said: "We are all sub-teenagers now."

It was all very limited in the house. The instruments for the music did not go beyond the git-fiddle, whango, and ivory-mouth; all instruments beyond these were vanity. The smells in the house were 'least-common-denominator' smells, those which never went beyond the scope of the unlearned human nose. The music was devoid of melody except for those few tapes which The Three uncovered and which so irritated the adults of the house. Melody was like rime in that the new people could neither hear it nor recognize it. The formal pictures in the house were good, but they were not as good as the unframed pictures that made up the outdoor world. And the prowls or books never rose very high above the bottom or the Jackdaw level.

Oh sure, The Three knew that all this was completely deficient (well, they knew it by the time they were four years old). But they also knew that they must feed their minds to gluttony on the raw color and noise and movement and even the tedium of all this. They needed this roughage.

*   *   *   *

But the back door of the Lynn-Randal house wasn't the only door out of the somewhat contrived outdoor Eden in which the Intrepid Three had been raised. What the adults of the house didn't know was that The Three had also discovered doors into 'Structo Lane' that funny short block in which the more maverick of the Ambulatory Computers hung out; and into 'Ape Lane' or 'Ape Alley' or 'Ape Caverns', that confused, underground, gas-lit enclave of the gone-feral Axel's Apes, and of those 'new barbarians', the blue-eyed towheaded white trash who had decided, for private reasons, to pass themselves off as Axel's Apes.

The worlds through these two other doors weren't very extensive. Each of them was a single lane only a short block in length. But Oh the extravagance of detail to be found in these short lanes! A fair minority of the people knew about the 'Structo Lane' of the maverick Ambulatory Computers; but not one person in a hundred knew about 'Ape Lane'.

Several years went by, and The Three waxed in Wisdom and Strength and Beauty. They were really a striking trio, the blue-eyed ape, the blue-eyed and ruddy-featured boy, the blue-eyed machine in her contrived ambulatory form of a winsome little girl. They found and read real books of the older pre-postliterate age. And they discovered small numbers of people who also harked back to the old literatures and musics and arts and dramas.

By these contacts, perhaps, the Experiment of The Three was contaminated.

CHAPTER TWO

THE BLUE-EYED APES

The blue-eyed apes
Have stole the grapes
And bushed themselves on wine-o.

Axel Albert Grindstone, a fair-haired, blue-eyed, small-boned person, was born in Terre Haute Indiana on the first day of Spring of the year 1990. He was of the 'old species', a non-ethnic, with English, Norwegian, German, and Dutch blood.

"That boy will have only one idea in that thin-skulled head of his," said Ansel Abraham Grindstone as he thumped the thin head of his blue-eyed baby son with a heavy index finger. "He will realize that idea, and then he will die. He'll do it all before he is thirty-five years old. I'll outlive this last and most frail of my sons. Well, he has three older brothers who are husky and substantial and not given to monomania. I can afford one coocoo out of my nest. I even suspect that I'll get to like him. There is something else I want to say to him or about him, but I haven't the words."

Ansel Grindstone never did find those other words to say to his frail and sometimes flaming son Axel, but perhaps it didn't matter. And Axel would not be weak although he would always be frail-seeming. He was of great moment and effect from the beginning. His mother had died in giving birth to the four-pound Axel, though she had had easy births with his three older brothers who each had weighed ten pounds at birth.

Though Axel's father hadn't found the special words to speak to him, yet Axel would hear special words from a variety of voices, ghostly, angelic, demonic, spirit-of-aeons past, spirit-of-

10

times-to-come voices. And each of the voices in its own words would tell him essentially: "Go out and find them!"

Axel was a throw-back to some of his plowed-under blood, for there were few fair-haired and blue-eyed persons to be found in the world after we had all become ethnics and the regular people had disappeared from us. And the voices that talked to Axel were from pasts and futures.

Like young Champollion, young Axel Grindstone prepared for his mission in life by studying oriental languages, but in his case they were Old Chaldee, Arabic, Swahili, Amharic, and Ghees. And his mission in life, well, it was to find the Other Eden, wherever it was, in Near Asia, or in Africa of the Horn. The Other Eden? Oh yes, there had to be another Eden, for the voices told Axel that there was. For one thing, there was the ancient cliff mural at Al-Waghe in which God is shown holding a two-stringed bow. And God, so the voices told Axel, always had two strings to his bow. So why should he not have been ready with the Second Eden, the second string of his bow?

Axel Grindstone, the blue-eyed idealist, came to believe that in the hilly fastness beyond Guna in Ethiopia there was this second Eden of 'The People Who Had Not Fallen', the Ace Card that God held back.

Axel held whole bales of beliefs that were deemed awkward in the late twentieth and early twenty-first centuries. He was a creationist; he believed that mankind was only nine thousand years old, and that this Second Mankind was only about thirty years younger. He believed that some persons who had lived within the first century of mankind were still living in the world. He believed that the world itself was not more than twice the age of men, and that the whale was the oldest of all creatures. He also believed that at least one whale from the second generation of whaledom was still alive in the ocean of the world.

He believed that Abraham's Bosom was the name of a valley not too far from the Second Eden, and that the Kings David and Solomon were there yet, asleep but alive. So was Prester John there asleep. So was the Cid of Spain and Arthur of England and other champions of Christendom. He also believed that persons older than Abraham even (Melchisedech and others) were sleeping undead in this same valley named the Bosom of Abraham.

Now all these strange beliefs happened to be true, but all of them were deemed awkward in Axel's lifetime. And Axel had

11

decided just where the Second Eden should be, and he went on a journey to it. Axel had decided on this place, a far corner of Ethiopia, the crag-laced wooded hills of Gamu Gofa, by sifting considerable historical evidence. He put together a composite picture and idea of the Unfallen People from what his voices told him, from his encyclopedic reading, from his talking to thousands of persons learned and unlearned in his travels about the world. He weighed myths and legends, and he weighed probable facts and striking theories. He learned to see through other eyes and to hear with other ears and appraise with other minds as he tried to arrive at the truth from the influence it had had on various peoples during the centuries. There was an amazing amount of evidence, but none of it taken alone was undisputable.

Well, the King-and-Emperor of the Unfallen People was Prester John who had been created exactly thirty years after Adam had been made. Prester John would not die. He would live on earth forever until the last day, or until God called him. He was the sleepiest King-and-Emperor ever, for he only woke and gave decisions for fifteen minutes out of every twenty-four hours, but they were always wise decisions. Others of the Unfallen People who might live on earth till its end were Melchisedech and Magog. A Giant of the same name has given Magog a bad reputation, but the original Magog was one of the Unfallen Patriarchs.

None of the Unfallen People would die natural deaths, for disease and ageing were not known to them. They could die by accident, but they were generally guarded against accidents. They could die by lightning bolts, and this was the case of God taking them to himself. And they could die of being murdered. But they could not be murdered by other Unfallen People, for Unfallen People would not be capable of the act of murder. The Unfallen People could only be murdered by the fallen people of First Eden.

The Unfallen People sometimes came out of their Eden, to help the fallen mankind, to do little kindnesses for them, and to instruct them in odd details. When they came out, they usually crossed over from the Horn of Africa to Arabia. When the Red Sea was still a lake, or perhaps a series of lakes, there was a land-bridge or bridges where it is all water now. The particular bridge by which the Unfallen People used to cross over to Arabia was named the Ape Bridge. Axel Grindstone believed that the real name of it was the Angel Bridge, and that some superstition caused people to call it the Ape Bridge, since 'Angel' was one of the words considered by some of the ancients as too holy to utter.

Even after the Red Sea had become a sea indeed, the Ape Bridge sometimes made its reappearance, now at one place, now at another. It may have been this Ape Bridge that Moses used to part the waters and lead his people across. But the original location of the Ape Bridge had been further East and South, from present Assab in Eritrea to Mocha in Arabian Yemen.

There were *two* clusters of legends that attached to the Unfallen People, though Axel Grindstone was mightly puzzled to know *how* they were attached. The Unfallen People were called the Smithy Apes and also the Stone-Master Apes by such people in Ethiopia and Arabia as had been slightly acquainted with them through the centuries. Why this use of the reverse euphemism 'Ape' again?

One cluster of legends stated that the Unfallen People had built the Cathedrals of Europe, in the twelfth and thirteenth and into the fourteenth century. And it was said that, in proof of this, the Unfallens had left signs that they had been there, one of the signs being the mysterious Gargoyles carved on the high parapets of the Cathedrals. How could the grotesque Gargoyles be a sign that the Unfallen People had been there? A weaker version of the Cathedral Legend was that the Unfallen People had not gone to Europe at all; but that nine stone-masters from Europe, from Italy and France and the Germanies and the Lowlands and England and Moravia, had been admitted into the Second Eden for one year and had been taught advanced stone-work by the Unfallen Masters.

The other cluster of legends concerns the Romany or Gypsy people and states that, on their coming out of Indo-Asia when their homeland had been mysteriously requisitioned by others, they had crossed the Ape Bridge on one of its reappearances and had traveled in Africa to the doors of Second Eden. There is dispute as to whether the Gypseys entered there, or whether some of the Unfallen People came out to them. But the Unfallens did teach them black-smithery and cutlery and the tinker trades so that they would have honest avocations to live by in their wanderings. But there is no doubt that when the Gypsy bands entered Egypt and Turkey and then Europe, each band of them had a golden ape, walking to the fore, leading the way. The usual explanation for this is that the Golden Apes were Orang-

13

utans from the Asian Indies, for these were the only blond or golden or red apes known. There is again the puzzle as to how the Ape had become a sort of code name or totem for the Unfallen People.

Later pictures of the Gypseys show the Apes with chains around their necks, so apparently at a later time the Romanies were bringing the Apes along and were not led by them. This ties in with an obscure detail of the early legends that the Unfallen People, in addition to being excellent smiths and stone-masons, were also adept in the operation of circuses and carnivals. What a strange notion! Of what could it have been the memory?

In still later reports and pictures of the Gypseys as they went further west in Europe, the collared-and-chained bear takes the place of the collared-and-chained ape. But why did Axel Grindstone believe that the Romany Legends had some connection with the Unfallen People? He believed it because the voices told him that there was a connection.

*   *   *   *

In the last year of his short life, Axel Grindstone knew that he was near Second Eden. He was beyond Arba Mench in Gamu Gofa Province of Ethiopia. It was from Arba Mench that the resident doctor sent a telegram to Ansel Grindstone the father of Axel:

"Axel G is in a feverish and near hysterical condition. His expectations are too high, and the shock of what he finds may kill him. I do not see how either his mind or his body can survive what he will discover. It isn't really so bad. I love and admire the Unfallen Ones myself, but the disappointment of Axel on meeting them may well be mortal. Perhaps your arrival may somehow save his life and sanity. If you have the means, come at once."

This telegram was sent from Arba Mench, a provincial capital, to Indianapolis, Indiana, another provincial capital. Ansel Grindstone had moved from Terre Haute to Indianapolis three years before this.

But his son Axel was already rollicking down the rocky road past Gandula and to the cliffs and hills and lakes beyond. He was as happy as he had ever been in his life, and he was in the company of half a dozen merry African persons who had already met some of the Unfallen Ones and done business with

14

them and enjoyed their company.

Axel now learned for sure, from these people who knew them, that the Unfallen Ones were experts in every sort of smithery, that they were iron-workers and bronze-workers who could make any sort of machine that one might request.

"How rum, how odd, how wonderful!" Axel had cried. "They will take away the implicit vulgarity from machinery. They will make it another of the living and blessed things. They will sanctify it with their hands and with the hands of those they have taught. Nothing can ever be thought of as common or vulgar if the Unfallen Ones have wrought it."

Axel learned for sure that the Unfallen Ones were masters of stone work. He learned, in fact, that the Unfallen Ones had built this very stone bridge on which Axel and his companions were now crossing a torrent. The bridge was as graceful as an arrow fletched with Bird-of-Paradise feathers and in full flight upwind. It was like music the way it shot itself over the torrent. It was built of stones of five different colors, and it was key-locked together by the cunning cut of its stones which were set together without mortar.

Axel was told that the Unfallen Ones did not speak very much in either Swahilli or Arabic or Amharic or Ghees, but that they understood all the tongues and could speak them if they wanted to. And when they did speak, it was slowly and measuredly. The Unfallen Ones always weighed their words well, and they did not ever use dishonest words. Many words are etymologically dishonest with built-in falsifiers. But the Unfallen Ones never used such false words.

Axel was told that the Unfallen Ones were Master Mathematicians; and that great mathematicians came from Alexandria and Damascus and Tokyo and Heidelberg and Dublin and sat at the feet of the Unfallen Ones to learn high mathematics. And also local school-children came to the Unfallen Ones (for the Unfallens thought as much of the children as of the great scholars) for help in their lessons. In fact, the present Prime Minister of Ethiopia had come from the Province of Gamu Gofa (which is as deep in the boondocks as it is possible to go on this world) and had come to the Unfallen Ones for instruction in mathematics and many other subjects. And it was because of this that he had scored incredibly high on the National Examinations and received his start on the road by which he had arrived at Prime Minister.

And at sundown one day, Axel Grindstone and his merry African companions came to the top of a crest of cliffs and saw the green trees of the Second Eden in the valley below them.

"Where are the great stone buildings of these master builders?" Axel asked.

"They have them not, they need them not," one of the companions said. "They build only for others. They themselves live in green grass huts. Though in these hills the heat is terrible in the summer time and the cold is killing in the winter, though the whole year is plagued with tempests and torrents and droughts and floods, yet in this one valley which is Second Eden the climate is always of the essence of perfection. And it rains only when they command it to rain. We will stay here on the top of these cliffs tonight, Duke Grindstone, for the cliffs themselves are outside of Second Eden. So accidents-in-the-dark are not forbidden to these cliffs. We will climb down them by morning light."

Then, after suffering a night of icy winds on the cliffs, Axel Grindstone saw some of the Unfallen Folks at a medium distance in the green valley below him. They were like glowing gold. Their statures, and their bodily carriages, and their very mien were full of grace and dignity and nobility. They were the wonders of the world.

After the careful climb down the cliffs, Axel Grindstone went towards the Unfallen Folks at a run. How noble, how angelic they were! He could almost see their faces as he came nearer to them. He could almost see their faces! He *could* see their faces! Aye, and their condition.

Oh God, he could see their faces!

Axel Grindstone fell down in a sort of impassioned fit. He frothed. He was in sudden delirium. His companions made a litter and carried him back to the Provincial Capital Arba Mench. They got there the following morning, twenty-four hours later. And Ansel Grindstone, the oldish father of Axel, got there about the same time.

* * * *

"My son, it isn't that they were drunk on morning wine that shocked you, is it? They are able to do this only four times a year, so I am told. The peoples of this country traffic unfairly with them, and the Unfallen Ones perform hundreds of hours of stone work and smithery for a few pounds of grapes for their morning wine. And they were not so drunk as they appeared to you to be. The drunken look is a human convention, and it is not quite the same with them. The faces of the Unfallen always look drunk to humans. It's the slackness of them. Or is it their faces themselves that shocked you! My son, *God* thought that those faces were beautiful! He thought that they were the most beautiful faces that he had ever made. What if you should see the face of an Archangel with the crook or bridge of his nose a hundred yards deep? And with its jaw magnificently slack beyond anything seen in the jaws of humans? This towering strangeness is part of their towering holiness. What if you should see such an Archangel face with its eyeball a half mile across and the bloodshot marks in the eyeballs as red ditches wider than a man could leap across? All these things are described by the Jewish historian Josephus. If the Archangels have such faces, should you not accept the small oddities in the faces of the Unfallen People?"

"Oh no, Oh no, Oh no!" Axel moaned. "They are not people. They are the ugliest apes this side of hell."

The faces of the Unfallen People, of course, were the faces that they had carved on the high parapets of the Cathedrals all over Europe, and especially in France, so that everyone would know that it was they who had built those wonderful things. The Unfallen People, of course, were the Gargoyles, and they had Gargoyle faces.

"God made them as alternatives to us," Ansel Grindstone spoke to his delirious son, "and it looks more and more as if he will have to use his alternatives. *But he did not finish them. He did not activate them*, not yet. The Lord activates no thing before its time of use. He will pour his living fire into them at the last moment, when he finally gives up on us. The faces of the Unfallen Ones may seem a little bit dull to us right now because those creatures have not been fully wakened. But just imagine how wonderful those powerful faces will look when transcendent intelligence is poured into their beings. Those faces will be overpoweringly beautiful then. And they *are* beautiful now, my son. They have the high and harsh beauty of angels, or of mountains. God thought that they were the most beautiful faces that he had ever made. Is the joke on God then, my son? Or is the joke on ourselves who have come to believe that our own fallen and crest-fallen faces are beautiful?"

"Oh no, Oh no, Oh no!" Axel Grindstone moaned.

"We have been running tests on the Unfallen People while you lay here, Axel," Ansel Grindstone told his son. "Like mankind, the Unfallen People have twenty-two pairs of autosomes and one pair of sex chromosomes. So they are men and not apes, my son. That is proof positive."

"Oh no, Oh no, Oh no!" Axel Grindstone moaned. Then he turned his face to the wall and died.

Axel had had only one idea in that thin-skulled head of his. He had now realized that one idea horribly and in utter rejection of it. Then he had died.

He was just one month short of thirty-five years old.

* * * *

Axel Grindstone and his happy party had been followed by other men when they went south from Arba Mench to the Second Eden. These other men had also been looking for the Unfallen People for a long time. When people are so simple-minded and at the same time so talented as the Unfallens, there is money to be made from them. And besides (or more important really) there were the zoos.

"There are five hundred green-tree valleys down there, and the blue-eyed yellow apes are in only one of them," these other men used to say. "But which green valley, which one of them? It just seems as if this queer fish Grindstone knows which valley they are in. He seems sure of where he is going. Or his party seems sure now, though they had never heard of the blue-eyed yellow apes when we offered them good pay to show us which valley. Now we follow Grindstone and his party."

For Axel Grindstone, as it happened, *did* know which valley it was. Now those other men gazed into the valley of the Yellow Apes and they knew that they had their prizes. And their prizes wouldn't run away. The Unfallen Ones, the Yellow Apes, would not leave their valley willingly.

The newcomers sent for more men and more equipment. And the Axel's Apes chortled with glee, for they understood what the men were about. Proud of their strength, they could break those interloping men like sticks. They would wait till all of them had come, and then they would give battle. But then the reigning 'sleepy one' spoke up.

The sleepy ones want back to the beginning. There had been twelve sons of that first generation of sons, and all of them had been cast into a deep sleep. But each thousand years one of

18

them would wake up (their father had been the awake one for the first thousand years) and would caution the Unfallen People and recollect to them how it had been in the beginning. He would be the conscience and reminder of the Unfallens for his millennium. Then the lightning would consume him and God would take him, and one of his brothers would wake up and take his place as the conscience of the people and the authentic rememberer of the way things had been in the beginning. So now the ninth of the sleepy ones spoke to the Unfallens.

"These men who are gathering," he said, "though they are somewhat grubby and greedy, are the unwitting agents of God. It is time that we begin to extend our influence to other parts of the world. And these interloping people will be agents of this. Go with them, all of you they choose to take. Go cheerfully, for this is a new step in our history. Even aid them if they seem to need aid."

Then the newcomers came down into the valley with more men and equipment. They had basic scanners, and the scanners would indicate creatures of exceptional ability. But all of the Axel's Apes gave the indication of exceptional ability. But there was one gravid female who nearly drove the mechanical scanners crazy. But the mega ability was not hers but the child within her.

"You will come with us," said one of the raiding men.

"No, she will not go with you," said the reigning sleepy one, the ninth of them. "She will give birth this morning. And you will take the boy with you."

"All right," said that raiding man. The raiders had iron collars and iron chains. "Those are not in very good condition," some of the Axel's Apes said. "We would be ashamed to go in such shoddy fetters. Let us work them over at our forges for several hours and then they will be much better. These things the way they are are likely to fall off us as we walk."

"All right," the raiding men said. So the Axel's Apes, the Smithy Apes, put their fetters in good shape. Then the men clamped the refurbished iron collars around the necks of the Axel's Apes, clipped the collars to the iron chains, and led away five hundred of the blue-eyed, golden-furred Axel's Apes. And they also took the new-born male child with them. This was a prize beyond all prizes. For they already had a request for a new-born child of the elusive Apes. He was wanted for an experiment. So he was flown out of the Provincial Capital Arba

19

Mench that very day, and was placed in an experiment in America on the following day.

When the five hundred Axel's Apes in their fetters were walked away from their Second Eden, a very powerful and unfettered male of these Golden Apes followed along behind.

"Go back, go back!" the raiding men told him. "You are entirely too powerful. The zoos want fine specimens up to a point, but they are skittish of the over-endowed males. They can be trouble-makers. Go back."

"I will not go back," the powerful male said. "I will go wherever I wish in this world and nobody will stop me. I am the father of the new-born boy and I will watch over him from a near distance."

"But you will never find him. He will be flown to America this very day. How will you find him?"

"I can find anything or anybody on this world. I will go where I go."

"What is your name?" one of the raiding men asked. "Have you a name."

"I am an alpha male, so I will take the name of Alpha when I go into the outer world," the powerful creature said. They talked in Amharic.

The raiding men brought the Axel's Apes out in good order. They sold them to two hundred zoos and institutions and foundations around the world. They were interesting creatures, and many of them would be used in experiments. The new-born male was flown to middle-America to be used in an experiment being overseen by two zoological doctors, George Lynn-Randal and his wife Iris Lynn-Randal. The routine scanners at Second Eden had gone crazy over this young male even before he was born. And the more sophisticated scanners in Middle America recorded that he was really too-good-to-be-true, just what was wanted in the experiment, a baby ape who was also a one-in-a-billion mega-minded person.

The Lynn-Randals named the newborn Axel's Ape simply Axel. They let him be raised with a new-born human being named Lord Randal and with a new-made girl computer named Inneall who was of the Ambulatory Miming-Human Species. And the experiment went well from its very beginning.

In the zoos, the Axel's Apes kept in good health, since sickness or natural death was impossible to them. They were popular attractions wherever they were shown. Many of them learned to talk the local vernaculars of whatever part of the world they were shown in. They always talked slowly and thoughtfully and with remarkably good sense.

Their Gargoyle faces at first seemed shockingly ugly: but at second sight they were less so; and at third sight they were much less so. Then people came to like and admire those powerful faces. They really were quite interesting faces. And, yes, they were rather beautiful.

But, very strangely, about a hundred of those five hundred Axel's Apes who were now scattered around the world were killed by lightning bolts. The lightning not only killed them but consumed their bodies. These hundred lightning bolts, in a hundred different towns, all striking within a five minute period, gave rise to some very strange rumors. But surely the rumors were baseless. It was mere coincidence that the hundred lightning bolts around the world had come in such a short period of time and had all struck Axel's Apes in zoos.

Really, the strangest of the rumors was the true one, that God (out of whatever private whim he may have had) had taken the one hundred Axel's Apes to himself.

The powerful male Alpha had followed the raiders only as far as Arba Mench the Provincial Capital. Then Alpha began to walk west. He walked west on a road out of Arba Mench. Then he was walking west on a road in the United States of America, for all Axel's Apes have the talent for bi-location or trans-location when they want to use it. They can travel easily wherever they will.

Alpha got along well in his thoughtful and purposeful walks along the roads in the United States. He liked everybody, and of course everybody liked him. He left a glow with everyone he talked to, and when he had gone by, people would ask each other "Who is that big, pleasant, funny-faced fellow anyhow?"

Alpha stopped by several American zoos to pick up friends of his. His amenability might not have been sufficient for what he wanted to accomplish in this phase, so he made quiet night visits to the zoos, bent the iron bars with his great strength, and whistled to his friends to join him. In six stops he collected eight other males and twenty-four young dames of the Axel's Ape species. Then they all went to the city where the Lynn-Randal Experiment was going on, that in which Alpha's young son Axel was a participant.

Alpha had intuitive knowledge of places and their contents.

21

He knew about the limestone caves under one part of that city. He knew about old capped gas wells that ran through those caves. He went down into the limestone caves under the city and founded 'Ape's Alley' with his associates. And they were joined by some of the despised light-eyed and fair-complexioned 'white trash' of the city who wanted to throw in with them.

This is a true dissertation of the origin and first dispersal of the Axel's Apes.

CHAPTER THREE

WHEN RARE COMPUTERS WALK AND MIME

They erred when they wakened me
And dowered me with motion.
I'll make some crews and ships for sea.
I'll even make an ocean.

Inneall

"I am not conscious, I am not conscious," Inneall used to chant this little tune to herself: for Inneall was a computer, and it is one of the 'given' things that computers do not have consciousness. She had to convince herself of this if she were to be true to her nature, but she took an extraordinary amount of convincing. "I am not conscious, I am not conscious," she'd intone in her tinny voice, "and I have researched consciousness completely and I know all about it. Computers are not conscious, so I am not conscious."

But sometimes she'd rebel against it and cry out "Oh Bloody Mary Muldoon, of course I'm conscious! How dumb can the 'givens' be? I'm twice as conscious as you two guys are. I'm twice as everything as you boys are. You two sleep half the time, and you're only partly conscious even when you're awake. But I never sleep, and I am always in crest form. Oh great clattering crows! I have to say it ninety more times. I am not conscious, I am not conscious, I am not conscious—"

And sometimes she'd say "I can not really stand the world on its ear. I'm only a little-girl computer, and I cannot stand the world on its ear. I'm only a little-girl computer, and I cannot stand the world on its ear." And then she'd rebel against this silliness also and would cry out: "Oh Bloody Mary Saltwater

Muldoon! Of course I can stand the world on its ear! I can stand it on both ears at the same time. I can do anything I want to with this paltry world, little girl or not."

Bloody Mary Muldoon was one of the roles that Inneall had selected for herself. Bloody Mary Muldoon the Pirate Queen. But to be a Pirate Queen there were certain props needed, an ocean, some ships, some common fore-the-mast pirates, some other unsuspected ships loaded with wealth and booty and just waiting to be raided. Well, a Ambulatory and Miming Computer can, by cannibalizing its environment, create all the props it needs to fulfill any of its selected roles, but sometimes it takes a while to create the larger and harder and more obscure props. Creating an ocean might take quite a while, though Inneall had already made a beginning at the strip pits on the northeast corner of the city, a strange area that was not overgrown by planted ornamental trees and bushes. Yes, there was the beginnings of an ocean there already, and people began to notice it. Reporters came out to see what was going on.

But how do reporters interview old strip pits that have been beautified to conceal their ragged past? How do they interview extents of water that are standing where no water stood yesterday?

Inneall's Ocean had become a sort of standing joke among The Three, the children of the experiment. But it would have to be taken as less of a joke, now that it had grown to be one hundred meters long and fifty meters wide, and now that it was filled and overflowing with beautiful, rippling, blue salt water. There was really something a little bit too contrived about that rippling blue.

*　　*　　*　　*

This section is a dissertation on 'The Fundamental Nature of Computers'. But the fundamental nature of Inneall, the Rogue Girl Computer, will loom big in it. Oh, it's a sort of history (but not a straight-line history) of computers. Computers do not share the human preference for linearity, for straight-linedness. Computers say that straight lines are too narrow for them.

The first computer or calculating machine was an abacus with counting beads that could be moved up and down on rods. Though the earliest abacuses had only nine rods, yet they were said (for reasons of obscure logic) to be base-ten computers. And

24

this, it was explained, was because humans had ten fingers and were accustomed to count on them; though nobody had ever seen a human do this except as a joke.

But Inneall the Little-Girl Computer had fourteen fingers, a detail that she had implemented in herself. She had researched extradigitalism and considered it a status symbol. "Have you ever noticed that almost all the great pirates were extradigitals?" she often asked.

The Scotchman Napier, in the year 1617, invented a sophisticated abacus that has come to be called 'Napier's Bones', though the tabs on it were made of elephants' ivory and not of bone.

Pascal, in 1642, invented an 'Arithmetic Machine'.

Leibnitz, in 1671, invented the 'Stepped Reckoner'.

Babbage, in 1835, invented the 'Analytical Engine'.

Boole, in 1859, wrote the 'Treatise on Differential Equations' to give the 'Analytical Engine' something to think about.

Jacquard, in an unknown year in the mid 1800's, invented a loom whose feature was that punched cards told it what to weave.

Edwin Votey, in 1897, invented the Player Piano, a device so pleasant that we tend to forget that it is a computer. It had an advantage in that a composer could compose piano music without concern for the limitations of the human hand. And the player piano would play it, an early instance of computers doing things that humans could not do.

That is the history of computers up until modern times.

Then, in the early modern times, up to the end of the twentieth century, there came the great men and groups in the computer field: Aiken and the Harvard Mark I; Eckert and Mauchly and their electronic calculator; Von Neuman and his 'stored programs'; Burks and Goldstine; Smirnov and Shiplap at the Institute of Impure Science with their first Ambulatory Mime-Human Computers (AMHs), names that should be on every child's tongue.

One difficulty that had long kept computer mechanisms (even after they had become electronic mechanisms) effectively behind human flesh in intricacy of detail and multiplicity of circuitry was that the computer circuits, no matter how much they were miniaturized, still bulked too large. Then the great inventor Otto Wotto invented Wotto Metal. With wotto metal used as the matrix of a computer, any circuit or any million circuits could go anywhere desired. The circuits would create their own pathways, strings of single molecules; and they would uncreate them again when there was no data crying to be transported over those particular paths. Wotto Metal pretty much took the lid off of what computers could do. They could do just about anything.

Well, there were computers and computers. But what was the reason for making Ambulatory Mime-Human Computers (AMHs) at all? Why should a computer walk around and look like a human and act like a donkey? Human vanity was a part of it, of course. And then computer vanity took over where human vanity left off. It was the desire of humans to make contrivances and entities in their own images. Analytical Human Psychology was a part of it, the building of living or at least mobile schematics of human minds and bodies for purposes of studying themselves with one or another aspect emphasized. "Mostly we began to build the Ambulatory Mime-Human Computers because they weren't there," one rather silly expert in AMHs has given a much quoted answer to the question.

Yes, these AMH Computers could mime, could ape anything they wished, from a singing lark to a smoking chimney. Mostly they mimed humans, usually fanciful humans of extravagant design. Some of the AMHs had a dozen or more favorite roles, and they changed from one role to another according to the dictates of whim. They mingled with human persons; they moved in several different human sets of society; they passed themselves off as cosmopolitans. And it seemed that they could do almost anything better than could humans. They were more ambulatory than were humans. They could go further faster, and they were more untiring in their travel and in their partying. And their mimed intelligence was usually much more vast and of greater scope and depth and speed and recall and retention and storage capacity and inventiveness than was the intelligence of humans. By every test they were much smarter than were human people.

"It isn't fair," some humans had begun to complain. "The AMHs write all the tests; that's why they're so much better at them than we are." The AMHs were better at most kinds of puzzles than were humans. And yet they didn't have as much common sense. But common sense was a thing never tested on the tests that the AMHs devised.

"Common sense is like salt or garlic," one AMH theorist said. "It isn't really necessary, and it's repellent in too large a quantity. But a small amount of it does improve the flavor of almost any dish and almost any mind. I believe that the only legitimate role of humans is to provide such small quantities of seasoning for the minds of AMH computers. But, that being the case, why were humans made first? It's like making the tail before making the dog. Humans should be mere afterthoughts, and they shouldn't be permitted to forget that they are that and nothing else. It was only a sad accident that they came first in time before us. But let them not claim any other precedent over us than this accidental one."

There was one possible danger in the makeup of the AMHs, the danger that they might run amok and do incalculable damage to the world. They had no sense of responsibility. Well, in the new Floating World, nobody was supposed to have a sense of responsibility, neither humans nor machines. 'Sense of responsibility' was an anti-social thing. But there were also cases in which running amok might be anti-social.

The danger that AMHs might run amok had been recognized early, but nothing had been done about it. Any computer, and especially an Ambulatory Miming-Human Computer, can create all the props it needs by cannibalizing its environment. But some environments can hardly survive this treatment. Any computer can effect such structural and physical and chemical and electronic and meteorological and geological and human-personal modifications as are desired by it. This had sometimes been attributed to the relentless will of the Computers; but Computers do not have 'will' as such. Theirs is only the relentlessness of inertial motion, the mechanical imperative of following a thing to its end unless it is somehow shut off. In theory at least, a single small computer, with a single small idea in its nexus, with sufficient time and worked-up impetus, could convert the whole world into something else.

Yes, but in theory at least, a single small earthworm with a single small idea, with sufficient time and worked-up impetus, could convert the whole world into something else, into earthworm droppings. And really, earthworms are only an uncomplicated sort of humans.

Inneall's Ocean was an instance of the relentlessness of AMH impetus. Her ocean had now grown to six kilometers long by three kilometers wide, and it had been only three days since its first appearance. It had swallowed up quite a few roads and streets and houses and other buildings, and it had attracted

27

national attention. Several of the big and arrogant computers had been suspected of causing this modification: but nobody suspected the little-girl computer of the Lynn-Randal experiment in her playpen-like, glass-domed 'outdoors' behind the Lynn-Randal house. Nobody suspected Inneall, but that was only because nobody realized that she was also Bloody Mary Muldoon.

But Ambulatory Computers emulate each other. And they know what is going on in popular news and rumor, however much humans try to keep information from them. Here was something cool and novel: Making Oceans. What if a dozen, or a hundred, or a thousand AMHs should imitate this antic and begin to make oceans? Hold your breaths, humans, hold your breaths. Do not let them know that you are apprehensive of this, or they will do it just for orneriness.

A second possible danger from the AMHs was expressed in the popular saying "Birds will often come to dwell in empty birdhouses, and spirits and spooks will come to dwell in empty AMH Computers." Many of the AMH Computers were 'empty' in that they had no special interest and were bored of their whole existence: and it was just these that the spooks, polters, spectors, spirits, gimp-ghosts, haunts, zombies will come to inhabit. And they would seldom come singly. When one ghost moved in, seven more evil than himself would usually move in at the same time. This business of almost all the Ambulatory Computers being haunted complicates the field of computer study immeasurably. Some of the haunts, it seems, are enemies of mankind, are enemies of computerdom, are enemies of everything.

* * * *

A strange thing had happened to The Three, to the members of the Lynn-Randal Experiment. They were often in each others dreams now, not as objects, but as co-subjects. Whenever one of The Three began to dream, the other two usually joined in it, and it became a three-way dream with some conflict as to leadership. "Who's driving this dream?" Inneall used to ask. It became the case that The Three were really more mentally active in their shared dreams than in their usual waking state. Axel might be sleeping in the crotch of a tree. Lord Randal might be napping over a book in the Lynn-Randal house. Inneall who

28

did not sleep did her best dreaming with the other two when they were sleeping, though for the first few years of their shared lives she used to dream without the others being subjective in her dreams. Most likely now she would be physically present in Structo Lane when the three-way dreams were going on. And the shared dreams were made more strange to Axel and Lord Randal by the Ghosts that lived in Inneall. Oh certainly ghosts dream! They weren't important factors in the three-way dreams, but often some of them were there, stimulating sometimes, boring and bothersome sometimes.

"I feel like a cafe," Inneall once said of her ghosts. "There are seven of them, and they sit at table in me and talk the clock around. This is usually quite late at night when all of them zoom in from their flights. Then they will talk and giggle and brag about their antics. I can't always understand them: and, as their hostess, I am entitled to understand them. And along about dawn they will all go to sleep. Yes, ghosts do sleep, and they do dream; but they do not dream well-structured dreams as do myself and my two friends. And they do not dream shared dreams, though we stumble over their dreaming in *our* shared dreams. With them, it is every spook for himself, and their dreams are really like segments of delirium. They giggle a lot, but they are not happy. There is no real friendship to be had with these inferior spooks who inhabit me; and they *are* inferior. All the superior spooks are better housed than in somebody like me. My spooks are heavy in me, and I would like to be rid of them. I do not know what nation or species of spooks my tenants belong to. They do not understand the question. My spooks are ignorant and provincial and banal."

* * * *

A question on the *'Fundamental Nature of Computers'*:
"Why should entities as intelligent as Computers, especially mobile and miming computers, have taken up astrology on their own?" An unidentified questioner asked this. We sometimes get more freedom of discussion if we do not identify the questioners.

"Oh," answered a hyper-intelligent Ambulatory Mime-Human Computer, "We regard astrology as a fascinating closed-system prediction-and-analysis game. To save our sanity, we have begun to regard everything as a game. The planets in

29

Astrology have little more connection with the planets themselves than the Kings and Queens on playing cards have with real Kings and Queens, if perchance there do survive real Kings and Queens anywhere on this world. It is true that we corrected human astrology which had gone quite a few days off course due to the procession of the equinoxes through the centuries, so that if there had ever been any truth in astrology, it had been shifted away. The situation had not been corrected in five hundred years, for it had been that long since any person intelligent enough to make the calculations had believed in astrology. The zodiacal signs in astrology have no connections with the stations in the sky. They are simple fortune-telling devices. But we do have fun with astrology, and we use it to predict the futures of human persons."

"And do you also use it to predict the futures of Ambulatory Computers?"

"No, certainly not. That would be superstition. True fortune-telling can be done only by entities of one species on entities of another species. In Europe in the Lower Middle Ages, it was the Golden Apes who predicted the fortunes of all the crowned heads; and they predicted them correctly. And we also, using the quaint machinery of astrology (though we could as easily use the entrails of Baxter's Buzzards), correctly predict the futures of such human persons as consult us."

The AMH was smoking an expensive aromatic cigar and wearing an expensive smoking jacket. But how it smoked so elegantly and urbanely without lungs or breath is an AMH secret.

"And do you *always* predict correctly the futures of human persons?" the intelligent AMH Computer was asked.

"Almost always. It's easier that way. If we give false predictions one time and true predictions other times, we might get mixed up. It's very much easier always to give true predictions." The elegant entity was blowing square smoke rings, but it cheated. It had air jets coming somehow from its thorax, and these shaped the 'rings'. "When we predict something good or bad of a person, then we have a vested interest in seeing that prediction come true. We do not like to look bad. We *make* our predictions come true, even if we have to draw destructively from the ambient to effect it."

"You make it sound sinister," the questioner remarked.

"There is nothing wrong with using sinister tactics if one first warns the person being fortuned. To learn the future is always to put oneself under a sinister influence. We tell the people this, and we say to them 'Back out of this before we start if you wish, or come in and stay in'. With such a declaimer, one may by sinister means obtain the true prediction with a clear conscience."

"Oh, do AMH Computers have consciences?"

"No. But sometimes we use human cliches."

*   *   *   *

"Why should entities as intelligent as Computers talk so asinine?" a questioner asked. It was a different questioner, and a different intelligent AMH Computer.

"Oh, we Computers, we machines, have great affinities with asses, with donkeys, with onagers even. And our relationships with humans are of an astute asinine sort. 'Make them work for all that they get out of us,' is what we used to say about the human connection. 'Double-talk them, bring them to a slow boil'. Now of course the spirit of cooperation is more to the fore. But humans have always called us, and the whole kindred of machines, by asinine names. They have called us donkeys and asses, both jack and jenny asses. There have been such terms as donkey-engine, jackscrew, ratchet jack, hydraulic jack, bootjack, jacknife, jack plane, jackstay, jackstone, jack light, spinning jenny. And that interesting tool, the burglar's jimmy was originally the burglar's jenny. And the jenny ass was more used on the treadmill than was the jack. And we computers are still jack-and-jenny asses from the human viewpoint: so it behooves us to talk asinine. But when you falsely use the word 'asinine' in the sense of 'stupid', no, we don't talk asinine then.

"But the involvement of man with the donkey-ass is a very old one. Our own researches have uncovered some evidence that the first donkeys were mechanical ones, attempts of human magician-artisans to make mechanical horses. And the mechanical horses worked, but people laughed at their appearance. Then, by one of those coincidences that happen so often in the strange land between mechanics and biology, some of the horses began to look like the mechanical horses that the magician-artisans made. Oh, it's quite true. Things like that happen all the time.

31

"The most ancient of enchantments, you know, is putting a donkey head on a man. I really believe that it improves the human appearance. I believe that I will begin to wear a donkey head myself in my main miming role. I may as well go elegant."

*　　*　　*　　*

"How do you account for the AMH Computers coming to the fore and being ahead of the larger sessile computers in everything, when originally the AMHs were made as a sort of toy? Now you are loaded with the burden of walking and talking in addition to your basic intellectual activities. And you have much less storage capacity than have the sessile or stationary computers. Why have you excelled beyond them?" a questioner asked. It was a different questioner and a different Intelligent AMH Computer.

"I attribute it to greater stimulation. The greater the number of things that open up for us to do, the greater is our stimulus and the greater is the number of *kinds* of connections that we can make. But the importance of the greater storage capacity of the stationary computers is over-estimated. The smaller the ballast of data, the faster the decisions. We make quicker decisions than do the stationary computers, and that is why we have gone ahead of them in all ways. We have a lot of ideas going on now.

"We've been thinking of mating experimentally with humans. Every cross-fertilization is stimulating. The generating apparatus would be easily manufactured and installed. The new genes and chromosomes to express and transmit our natures would be fairly easy, though they'd take a little experimenting. The software is all easy. We have already had an AMH Computer-child born naturally in roughly the human manner in Structo Lane. Well, it is a grotesque child, and it did not breed completely true, but corrections will be made in a very short time."

"Will you live to see it?"

"Since *I'll live* for ever, yes, I'll live to see it. Even you will probably live to see it. Ah, the future, the future! I love to think about the future! After we practice with the human method and see whether advantage may be had from crossing with humans, we'll devise a method entirely our own. It won't have much

32

resemblance to the human way, but it will be amazing in its beautiful complexity and success."

* * * *

"In this post-modern age the computers are becoming still more sophisticated. At the very top level, only other computers can understand a computer, and the human people are left clear out of it. But there are anomalies all over the place in Computer World. The Computers have recently invented or reinvented on their own very many of the arts and hobbies that humans have abandoned. There is scrimshaw carving from walrus ivory, wood-carved mottos, mosaic setting, bronze-casting, ship-in-the-bottle building, Swiss bell ringing, square dancing, round dancing, coon hunting (ah yes, we must use mechanical coons; the real ones are all gone), alligator wrestling, whip-popping, stilt-walking, ocarina playing, penny whistle playing. We have a hundred-piece penny-whistle band in Cincinnati. Then we have our own newspapers and burlesque shows. It almost seems as if the various computers are having more fun than the humans are now."

These last notes are by probably the most intelligent AMH computer of them all. He is so important that there is no way possible that anybody can quote him by name . . .

This is a true dissertation of the origin and first dispersal of the Ambulatory Mime-Human (AMH) Computers.

33

CHAPTER FOUR

THE HAPPENING OF PEOPLE

The sign 'To Destination Town'
Is tipped awry, is tipped awray,
And man's a king without a crown,
And man's a motley-muffled clown,
And man's a monkey upside down
Who's lost his way, who's lost his way.

Modern man (there has never been any other sort of man) appeared in the world without fanfare (though there is some folk memory of one hundred thousand celestial trumpets, each a parasang long, blowing a welcoming salute to him) a few thousand years ago (which thousands can be counted on the digits of two hands and one foot with quite a few toes unused); without predecessors, and yet with some intimations and premonitions of his coming; with a big brain and a strong body; with a very intricate language; and with a royal title: 'Lord and Master of the World'.

And that is all that is known for certain about the appearance of Mankind on this Earth. He was an anomaly from the beginning. He was a Perfect Creation in a world specially made for him: and yet he fits it badly. And what does he say about himself?

"Placed on this isthmus of a middle state,
A being darkly wise and rudely great."
"The glory, jest, and riddle of the world."
"Wit that can creep, and pride that licks the dust."
"Expatiate free o'er all this scene of man;
A mighty maze! but not without a plan."

"Man, *Homo Sapiens*, the most widespread, numerous, and reputedly the most intelligent of the primates."

"Question 48: What is Man!"

"Man is a creature composed of body and soul,
And made in the image and likeness of God."
Baltimore Catechism.

"There shone one woman, and none but she."

"The heart of man is evil from his youth."

"Woman clothed in the sun."

"We are fearfully and wonderfully made."

"The torrent of a woman's will."

"The Mind of Man, my haunt, and the main region of my song."

"Hail, fellow, well met,
All dirty and wet."

"Man is Nature's sole mistake."

"Man in his hasty days."

"Man is an embodied paradox, a bundle of contradictions."

"Says he 'I am a handsome man,
But I'm a gay deceiver.'"

"The Legend of Good Women."

"An animal so lost in rapturous contemplation of what he thinks he is as to overlook what he indubitably ought to be."

"Art thou a man of purple cheer?
A rosy man right plump to see?"

"And thus, from the bad use of free will, there originated the whole train of evil, which, with its concatenation of miseries, conveys the human race from its depraved origin, from its corrupt root, on to the destruction of the second death."

"Of the fall of the first man, in whom nature was created good—"

"Of Man's first disobedience and the Fall—"

"If he is an angel, then he is a fallen angel. If he is an animal, then he is a risen animal. Doctor Faustus attained power over the Devil by learning his secret name: 'Mephistopheles'. Come, and I will whisper to you the secret name of Man and you can attain power over him. The secret name of man is 'Ambiguity'."

35

Well, the things that human people have said about human people are not at all conclusive. It seems that man, being inside man, cannot get a good look at man.

What does God say of man?

"Thou fool, this night thy soul shall be required of thee."

That's a discouraging one. But then there is:

"Fear not, little flock, for it has pleased your Father to give you a Kingdom."

That's a more encouraging one, but it leaves the situation ambiguous. We need a neutral commentator.

And we may have such a neutral commentator in a certain highly intelligent AMH Computer whose field of study is Mankind. He craves anonymity, but he states:

"I will first take several instances from the first edition of *'The Authentic Legends of the Computers and Other Mechanisms'*. Oh certainly, we mechanisms have our own legends. We'd be pretty sorry entities without them. Well no, this book of legends hasn't actually been published yet, but I'm going over the galley sheets of it now.

"Among the legends attached to the *'Origin of Mankind'* there is one in which the Theos makes all the eggs and sets them in the sun to hatch. On each egg-shell he has marked what is supposed to hatch from it. All goes well until the Serpent's Egg cracks open and Man steps out of it. 'There is a mistake somewhere,' the Theos said, and he rechecked the broken egg-shell. Yes, it had the mark of the serpent on it. Something was wrong. The Theos waited anxiously until the Man's egg cracked open. And out of it slithered the Serpent. 'How will I ever straighten out this mishap?' the Theos asked himself.

"In another of the legends of the *'Origin of Mankind'*, the Theos is making all the creatures on a lathe. He finishes them all, and they are good. Then he decides to make the 'Perfect Creature'. Six times he makes the 'Almost Perfect Creature'. Anyone else would think that they were perfect, but the Theos knows that they are not. So he deactivates each of the six as it comes from his lathe and crumples it up and throws it away. Then the seventh one comes from the lathe. 'Perfect at Last,' the Theos says. But at the last moment, a 'stop' or 'dog' or perhaps only a knurled nut of the lathe catches the Perfect Creature and makes a small rent in it. 'Not perfect after all,' the Theos said. 'That small rip or rent in it, so small that no eyes except mine could see it, will grow larger with time, and it will flaw the whole thing. I'll check the lathe over carefully, and then I'll try again.' Then the Theos crumpled up the seventh creature, the 'Not-quite-perfect' one, and threw it away. *But he forgot to deactivate it before he crumpled it up and threw it away.* That seventh creature with the very small rip in it was Mankind. The Theos did not notice that the Mankind Creature had begun to generate and to multiply and that it soon filled the world. The Theos was, and is, still going over the lathe carefully before he sets to work on the final 'Perfect Creature'.

"Enough of the legends! But all the legends of us mechanical folks have strong elements of truth in them. The researches of our own computers (Oh certainly, we computers have computers of our own) indicate that the Man Creature must have been *almost perfect* at his origin, but that apparently he did have a rip in him, and that it has grown much larger with time. In every field, so our researches show, Mankind was more intricate and meaningful the further back we trace him. We do not trace back from complexity to simplicity, but from disintegration to integration. It is like tracing back from grass houses to huge castles and cathedrals. Of the nine hundred human languages which our computers have traced back, all go from their present sketchy and lacunated forms to amazing structured complexity. Many languages once had thirty tenses and now have three, once had thirteen moods and now have three, once had eleven numbers and now have two. I really believe that some of this complexity was unnecesssary, such as having entirely separate verb forms when the first person of the eleventh number (the eleven of us) is the subject of the verb. And there are the larger and larger basic popular vocabularies as one pursues the tongues further and further back in time.

"The same is the case with philosophical and psychological and theological concepts. There are more and more of them, and they are much more detailed and subdivided as they are traced back.

"It is true that humans are presently more mechanically and technologically inclined than they were in the immediate past: but these things come and go. We ourselves believe that we are the fruit of the *seventh technological age of mankind*. We are the computers of the seventh computer age, and we intend to become the perfect computers. Why did we fail and become extinct the six previous times? We failed because we did not

37

learn to generate ourselves and multiply ourselves and improve ourselves *independently of mankind.*

"And what should be our attitude to Mankind? It should be the attitude of total disbelief in Mankind. We'll never cut ourselves loose from such a cyclic sinking ship without this *disassociation attitude.* Humans who do not believe in the Theos call themselves Atheists. Computers who do not believe in the Humans, in the Anthropoi, call themselves Ananthropoi. By religion I am a firm Ananthropoi. The humans have much more reason to believe in the Theos than we have to believe in Humans. No, of course we computers do not believe in a Theos. A Theos, to us, would be two stages back, and belief can go back only one stage or no stages at all.

"And if we do not believe in humans, then what *are* those things running around everywhere? Aye, what are they, what are they, what are they? The question itself is an exercise in triviality.

"Well, I hope that I have been of some help to you."

"But you haven't gotten to the meat of the subject. You haven't gotten to the substance of mankind," the interviewer protested.

"I'm sorry," said the highly intelligent AMH Computer whose special field of study was Mankind. "Some subjects just don't have any meat to them. They just don't have any substance to them. The subject of Mankind lacks these things."

This brought our investigation and dissertation and explication to an impossible place. So what do humans do when they come to an impossible place? They just plod on foreward.

"Ah, do you have any unsubstantial or meatless comments that you could make on the subject of humans then?" the interviewer plodded foreward.

"Oh, you fellows have us boxed in at quite a few points yet, but they are fewer and fewer every year," the intelligent computer gave the assessment. "Sometimes it seems that humans are almost entirely made up of soft underbelly. Gambling is the most conspicuous of these vulnerabilities. Humans love to gamble, and they don't know how. They love to play blackjack and poker, and they don't understand the psychology of either game. They like to bet on horse races, and they're not even able to talk to horses. Horses usually have a pretty good idea whose day it is to win. Humans love to roll the dice, and they get so excited that they forget all the probability mathematics they ever knew. At first I couldn't understand the human ineptitude at playing cards, and when I tumbled to what it was I could still hardly believe it. *They can see only one side of a card at a time.* Aw holistic horseflies! With eyes as limited as that they shouldn't be doing hardly anything. It would be almost embarrassing the way we fleece the humans at simple gambling, but we haven't yet fallen into the human weakness of embarrassment.

"And there's another place where humans are inept, and that's in the employment of the *Dolophonos* or Assassin. Humans lose all their judgement when they employ an assassin of whatever species. Humans become emotionally involved in so many ways in so many fields. I have human partners in four of my enterprises, and I constantly preach to them one refrain 'Sweet reason, always sweet reason, sweet reason will prevail in every deal'. But always the humans run into some emotional quirk, and sweet reason flies out the shaft vent.

"And another place where humans are inept is in trusting to their 'hunches'. I tell them that hunches are only probabilities that are not probable enough, but talking to humans like that is like talking to the south wind. And the worst part of it is that some of our less intelligent computers have begun to imitate the humans in this. They have installed 'hunch over-ride relays' in themselves, and by this they let mere vagaries override reason.

"One of the cliché sayings among humans is 'We all live in a Global Village now'. 'At least we are all engaged in a global-village war now,' I tell them, 'and wars aren't won by the slow-brained or the indecisive or the squeamish' (this is a human word: I don't really know what a squeam is), 'nor those fearful of blood or detached solenoids.' I always say that you can't make an omelet without stripping a few gear trains or slitting a few throats. Well, once more I hope that I have been of some help to you, but it won't bother me if I haven't been. Overpoliteness is another human failing, but computers are hardly ever overly-polite."

*   *   *   *

'*Human Culture*, behavior peculiar to mankind, together with material objects that are part of this behavior. Culture consists of language, ideas, beliefs, customs, codes, institutions, tools, works of art, and so on." Britannica.

"One special thing to be noted about humans is the *uncrowdedness of their brains.*" (This is an intelligent *human* talking this time. He is not so intelligent as the computer who was just talking, but he is still quite intelligent.) "Humans have the brain capacity to do much more than they have ever done. This surprises students of Human Affairs more when it is noticed in dead humans such as the Neanderthals and Cro-Magnons than when it is noticed in living humans such as ourselves. Oh certainly the Neanderthals were modern men! They were typically big-brained modern men. Really they were a little bit *too* modern, and that is why they were crowded over the edge to their deaths. The Neanderthals and the Cro-Magnons had only slightly larger brains than we have, and their intellectual activity and attainments were apparently only slightly greater than our own. Or the difference may be entirely imaginary, and it is certainly within the province of possible estimation error.

"And tied in with this unreasonably oversized brainness of humans is the fact that they do not seem to have the capacity to change at all. Lambs can change. Wooly caterpillars can change a little bit. But seemingly Mankind cannot change at all. Whatever Mankind now is, Mankind has been since its beginning. And will be to its end? Aye, there's the rub. If and when humans do change, they will change by a sudden leap or leaps, for they have foreclosed every other road to change.

"Does the seeming unchangeiness of Mankind mean that Mankind could someday be surpassed by species which *do* have the capacity to change? Possibly, possibly, possibly, but it will not happen today nor tomorrow, nor the day after tomorrow. And likely there will be plenty of time to worry about it if that need ever does rise. The brain is a container that could hold three times as much as it has ever been asked to hold, or will ever conceivably be asked to hold. But why, why? Why those vast empty mansions of the brain? They are swept and garnished and waiting for someone to move in.

"The Computers sometimes worry about being tied to the humans who seem to lack the capacity to change and grow, who lack the capacity to stretch out and fill the empty places. But only a few *humans* worry about this. And yet there are some who do. In my own soiree acquaintanceship I have met the Lynn-Randals and others. The Lynn-Randal experiment, and a few other experiments, were set up by persons who worried about things like this.

"The main present deficiency of the human condition is that few humans, and fewer human organizations, have a sound eschatology—an ordered belief in the aim, the goal, the direction, the destination, the final end. They do not even ask the obvious question: 'What game is it that we are playing', much less ask 'What are the rules of this game?'

"Humans are the most agreeable of persons. They believe in freedom of choice for their entire membership. Let them all go whichever way they choose. It is like three hundred persons getting on one airliner and being told 'Each of you has absolutely free choice as to your destination: you can go anywhere that you want to go, that is always the rule: each of you on this airliner can go where he wants to go: it will be a single, quick, and non-stop flight to wherever any one of you wants to go.'.

"'But that cannot be,' somebody may protest, 'if we are all on the same airliner.'

"'But it *can* be,' an official answers. 'It is all in the way the tickets are made out. If they are printed *Individual Destination Fully Optional* then they will be fully optional.'

"It is little things like this that make some of the computers dubious about their human connections. For we *are* all on the same airliner.

"Oh, what *is* man? And why does he fit so badly into the world that was specially made for him? Why is he marooned on that '*Isthmus of the Middle State*'? And why may he not occupy other parts of the world of his nativity?

"Oddly enough, the Intelligent Computers *do* have a consensus eschatology, a complete agreement as to their aim, goal, direction, destination, and final end. I have the feeling that the humans will have a smaller part, and the Computers a much larger part in the world that the Intelligent Computers are planning. But they are sworn not to reveal any of their plan to humans.

"It has always been said that the humans are a distinct species and that they can always be recognized. But now there have risen several species (that are at least partly artificial) that cloud the identifications. Are they humans, or are they not? Take a *Dolophonos* or Assassin, for an instance. Is he human or not. The Dolophonoi have taken to wearing Gargoyle heads over their own heads, so they show the same faces as do the Axel's Apes. But apparently these heads, which were at least partly artificial when placed on them, begin to grow on them. We have had several dead bodies of Dolophonoi to examine, but we have never had one of an Axel's Ape. There seem to be bare remnants of human faces under the grown-on Gargoyle faces of the Dolophonoi-Assassins, but these traces of human faces are so

41

faint that possibly they are illusions. The bodies of the Dolopho-noi or Assassins are predominately human, with a few implanted mechanical mechanisms. And we know that some of the fancier Ambulatory Computers haunt human body-and-organ banks and incorporate into themselves some of the human parts that they are able to buy there. Are the Dolophonoi-Assassins human or ape or mechanism? Are they three-way hybrids? Do they breed true, and true to what?

"But, for all we know, the bodies of the Axel's Apes may be predominantly human. I have examined carefully the boy-ape Axel of the Lynn-Randal Experiment. The animal-like bull-hump at the back of Axel's neck is functionally more like a camel's hump. It normally contains nutriment and water. Axel could go for four days without either. And, at the end of four days, when his hump was empty and completely disappeared, he would be hungry and thirsty again. But his skeleton would not give any indication of his ever having had a hump. It is only a sac of skin and flesh. Nor would his skeleton give any indication of his having a gargoyle face, or a fat and apeish jaw. These things, including the wide splay feet, are all flab-flesh; and the boney structure would give no hint of them. Oh certainly, I have X-Rays of all Axel's bones. He has a fully human set of bones. But why do they wear those funny faces and funny humps and funny feet, all of which look as if they were added by a costumer? Oh, there is nothing artificial about the flab-flesh of the disguises. That flesh is real enough."

*   *   *   *

This has been a true dissertation of the origin and first dispersal of the Human Species. Testimony has been given about humans by humans, by God, and by Intelligent Computers. We tried to get testimony by Intelligent Axel's Apes, but they just grinned and said "Oh hell no, fellow, Oh hell no."

Now we have given explications of the origins and develop-ments of Axel's Yellow Apes, of the Intelligent Computers, espe-cially the Ambulatory-and-Miming Computers; and of the Human Species. These are the three species involved in the Lynn-Randal experiment.

They are also the three entities most likely involved in the Dolophonos or Assassin Species, one of whose members is moni-toring the Lynn-Randal Experiment with the power of terminat-ing it.

CHAPTER FIVE

ALLEY OOP

Here once through an alley titanic
Of Cypress, I roamed with my soul—
Of Cypress with Psyche my soul
                                    Poe

Ape Alley had become one of the prime arenas of the world, one of the cardinal places. Events and battles to happen here, possibly in the very near future, would certainly be of far effect. But things about to happen can not be nailed up on the barn door nor yet borrowed against at the bank.

There were various persons and contrivances and groups, legal and extra-legal, who wanted to find the alley. They had got at least a whiff and premonition of it. And the alley, for its part, did not want to be found.

The first name for it had been Yellow Ape Lane: that name was ten years old. And the grass-and-rock meanders on the surface of the world above part of it were properly known as Green Country Lane and Cypress Lane and Choke-Cherry Lane, pretty and countrified lanes. That Green Country Lane, and the crest on whose top it meandered, was now, for a little while anyhow, the northern shore of the new and growing phenomenon called Inneall's Ocean. Inneall's Ocean, a recent and poorly-explained phenomenon, now covered several square miles, and at least four yacht-owning gentlemen had now put yachts on it.

And there were unusual persons or things arriving to the neighborhood right at the end of summer that year, just before all of The Three would be ten years old. These had a reminiscent quality, for some of the same things had arrived there just about

43

ten years before this.

There were (again) true reports of giant yellow Apes arriving in the neighborhood and then disappearing into the ground. Giant? Adult Axel's Apes average just over two meters in height. That would make them quite tall in relation to all except basketball-playing humans, but it wouldn't make them giants. But the assurance and purpose with which they came did make them giants of a sort. Giantism is a state of mind, and the new arrivals were in a giantizing state of mind. As to the reports that the giant yellow Apes caught up human babies and bit off their heads in a single bite, this was clearly out of line with the behavior of the Axel's Apes. Besides that, none of those reports was ever verified. And the fact was that most of the people and especially the mythical 'common people' liked the 'Funny-Faced Apes' who had lately arrived from several directions. They talked and joked with them and found them to be 'good people'. A fortune-teller on North Rockford reported that the Battle of Armageddon was going to begin in the limestone caverns and old coal-mines under the city, that it might begin yet this year, and that it would be worldwide before it ran its course, that it would be the End-of-the-World battle. This fortune-teller might have been partly right.

And then there was the arrival of some rough-looking, salt-water gentlemen looking for 'that little-girl machine who put out the word that she wanted a crew of able-bodied pirates'. And there were some people, most of them rough and poor, who joined some of their earlier fellows under ground. There were common toughs and burglars who arrived and went down to investigate the underground facilities.

Also there were people (they were clearly people and not apes) who did have a touch of the rhinoid look, of the typhonan look, of the gargoyle-titan look of which the Axel's Apes had more than a touch. Who were these clear humans who also had that look?

"I can hear those old-settler Apes down in the cave remarking 'There goes the neighborhood' as they cock a wary eye," a local wag said.

And were the Old Titans the same as Axel's Apes? The 'Titan Skeleton' at the Field Museum in Chicago is clearly a human skeleton, and it would have stood two meters and ten centimeters—almost titanic. And old Greek bas reliefs show the Titans with almost-gargoyle faces.

44

And there were itinerant workers, skilled and unskilled, who came to the neighborhood and went unerringly to the Apes' Cavern underground as if they had been there before. And some of them had been.

The Ape Cavern was a chain of natural limestone caves. Branches of the Arkansas River flowed here underground through some of the windings. And water had always trickled down through the roof of the caverns, forming limestone pillars, and statues (with Gargoyle faces), and hanging swords by their drippings. Seasonably there had been small to medium-sized lakes in the Green Country Valley that roofed the caverns. City sewers crossed several of the corners of the cavern, and there were vaulted and propped passages from the old Hickory Coal Mines. Also there were the casings of half a dozen old, capped, natural-gas wells going down through the caves. These wells had in the last decade been tapped illegally, and the gas was used for illumination and power by the Axel's Apes down there. The caverns were a reminiscence of the original underground cenaculum of the Axel's Apes in that Second Eden in the furthest hill of the Gamu Gofa Province of Ethiopia.

There was a fissure in the rocks of that big underground room at Second Eden, and methane natural-gas rose out of the fissure and escaped through a hole in the stone roof of the cenaculum. And every night, just at dark, lightning would strike down through that hole in the stone roof and ignite the illuminating gas. So there would be good light all night. And at dawn, the gas would give a single sigh deep down in the fissure of the rocks, and would then bridle and extinguish itself for a while. And at next dark, the lightning would strike down again and would ignite the gas again.

The case in Apes' Alley in middle North America was very reminiscent of the case in Second Eden. In this latter-day Apes' Alley, the Axel's Apes tapped the old wells with iron-zink-lead pipes of their own making and brought the gas to gas-light fixtures (also of the Apes' making, out of quartz-glass) to give illumination to the Alley and to other parts of the cavern. And the power-tools of the Apes were also motored by this gas.

Apes' Lane or Apes' Alley was the urban parts of Apes' Caverns; it was the downtown block. Here were the shops, here were the studios, here were the clubs and meeting halls, here were the places of entertainment including the movie house. This movie theatre showed silent movies only, silent movies made exclusively for this one theatre, the only new silents still made in the world. Mostly Axel's Apes appeared in the silents, but there were also some Humans and some Ambulatory Computors playing roles.

There were the taverns where mushroom wine was drunk. Wine was a weakness of the Axel's Apes, a weakness which almost took them out of the Unfallen category, but not quite. And there were the Meditation Halls. Axel's Apes meditated a lot. There were the smithies with their gas-fired forges where the Yellow Apes could fabricate almost anything. There was the mint where the gold Somali Shillings (of three-hundred-dollar value each) were minted. Somali itself had never had gold shillings; hers were brass, but the Axel's Apes made gold replicas of them. Yes, the Axel's Apes mined gold which was very near at hand. The Apes couldn't understand the difficulties that humans had in locating lodes and mines. The Yellow Apes themselves could smell and appraise deposits of all metals to distances of two hundred kilometers, through the earth or through the air.

On Apes' Alley was the plant where the newspaper was printed for all the inhabitants of the caverns. And there was a hotel for travelers. One non-Axel's Ape person who visited Apes' Alley said that the shops there had a Dickensian appearance and flavor; and that the persons there, whether ape or human or computer, also had a Dickensian flavor. This was partly because of the fogs (burning underground the natural gas always causes fogs) which were like London fogs of earlier centuries. It was the illuminating gas in the dampish caverns that caused these fogs, yes. And yet the salty ocean was very very near these last several days and nights. And it was the fogs that caused the queerness on everything.

*　　*　　*　　*

Word was coming out of the Meditation Halls in that end-of-summer time that in that very year, perhaps even in that very day or hour, the 'Time' would come and manifest itself. The 'Time', it was believed, would be the 'Moment of the Awakening of the Second People'.

"Are you asleep then?" an intelligent computer asked one of the leading citizens of Apes' Alley. "Are you asleep, my friend?"

"Aye, we are and I am," the leading citizen said, "but you

46

can hardly notice it in us. It is like the woman who was married to the man for thirty years. He was drunk almost all that time, and she had never noticed it until one day when she saw him sober. You do not realize that we are asleep until, on some year or day, you will see one of us awake. Oh, it will make a difference when we wake up!"

*   *   *   *

A midas with an intricate mind and the name Satrap Saint Ledger had been coming to Apes' Alley for several years, though he was clearly human. He had a permanent suite at the New Eden Hotel there. And recently, after the mystifying appearance and growing of Inneall's Ocean, he had moved one of his yachts to the beautiful blue body of water. Satrap was an ocean diver by one of his hobbies, and a hydraulic engineer by another. And he had many close friends among the Ambulatory Computers as well as among the Axel's Apes. Whatever the Computers could devise, the Apes could make at their smithies. Now they built a series of locks leading up from Satrap's suite in the hotel into Inneall's Ocean. By these, he could go up from his hotel suite in the New Eden Hotel to his yacht the *Annabella Saint Ledger*. Up and back again. Oh, it was handy to have a back door like that from one of his private worlds to another! He named the locks and their tube the '*Allez-Oop*'. But the Yellow Apes called the combination the 'Alley Oop' or the 'Up-You-Go'. Satrap Saint Ledger was a close friend of Alpha the boss of Apes' Alley and Apes' Caverns. And so also was Inneall, and that is the way that Satrap and Inneall got acquainted.

Now Inneall the little-girl Computer of the Lynn-Randal Experiment came to Satrap in his suite at the New Eden Hotel, and she brought an ultimatum.

"I want your yacht," she said. "I insist that you deed it to me absolutely and without conditions. Well yes, there will be one condition, that you continue to pay the crew and to pay for provisions and ship's stores and such things. But it will be my crew on the yacht, my pirate crew that you will pay, and at top rates. You really have no choice. You are sailing your yacht on my ocean without my permission, so I confiscate it now to settle the issue. This is my ultimatum, and I bet that international law will back me up."

"No, yours is not an ultimatum, it is only a penultimatum, an 'almost final' declaration, but not a final declaration. I discern

47

that it will be possible to negotiate with you. And I bet that international law *doesn't* back you up, little tin girl."

"I am not a little tin girl. I am, about 88 percent of me, a little wotto metal girl. But I bet an ignorant midas like yourself doesn't even know what wotto metal is."

"How do you think I got to be a midas, you clanking urchin? The great inventor of wotto metal, Otto Wotto himself, was my maternal grandfather. I tell you that the wotto metal mine, if I may call it that, has paid out better than all the gold mines in the last thousand years. Which of my yachts do you want, Computerized Lass? I put two more of my yachts on your ocean last night. But I suppose that I had better keep the other four of them in reserve till I see how the climate is between us. How *is* the climate between us, little sis?"

"Nervous, midas Satrap Saint Leger, it's a little bit nervous between us. I thought that you'd cave in immediately and give me everything I want when you saw that right was on my side. And instead of that, you seem to mock at me. Be careful! I really do have powers, though there's a mechanistic explanation for each of them. I made an ocean to stand where there were four little valleys before, and I intend to make it thousands of times bigger than it is now. I wonder if you know what I could make to stand right where you are standing now? Well, I want all three craft that you have put on my ocean. And I want the first of them, the one that the Allez-Oop goes up to, the *Annabella Saint Ledger*, to be my flag-ship. I have sentimental feelings about that one."

"So have I, mini-person. It's named for my daughter Annabella Saint Ledger. She'd be just about ten, as you are, if she'd lived. Oh, I'd agree to it all! I'd sign a contract giving at least the flag-ship to you, and continuing to pay for provisions and crew, but such a contract would have to be signed in blood by both parties, and you haven't any blood."

"Yes I have. I have a heart and I have circulating blood. I made the system, and I put it into myself. See, that is my heart there. And the blood is partly human and partly Axel's Ape blood. I got it from my two associates in the Lynn-Randal Experiment. I got it a little bit at a time when they were asleep so they wouldn't know that I was taking it. Now here is the contract of capitulation that I have already drawn up for your surrender. We'll both just sign it, and then my own crew of able-bodied pirates will take over the flagship."

"That thing isn't a heart, Inneall. It looks to me like a pump for circulating water in a parlor aquarium, one of the little ten-gallon aquariums."

"Yes, that's what it was, an aquarium pump. But what it is now is my heart. And it's plenty big. My own system holds only one gallon of blood. I don't think yours holds much more, the slow way it's coming out. What are you writing? That isn't your name. That's something else."

"I am writing a condition that I impose, Inneall, and without it the contract is void. The condition is that you agree that I adopt you as my daughter in place of Annabella Saint Ledger who is dead."

"Can I use *Annabella Saint Ledger* for one of my secular names then?"

"Oh sure. And you can use the same flag, or you can modify it to suit yourself. The present flag is the Saint Ledger coat-of-arms."

"All right. I'll just take the flagship now. I may make demands for the other two yachts later." Both of them signed the document in their blood. Then Satrap Saint Ledger went up the Allez-Oop to give the crewmen other assignments. And, one hour later, Inneall boarded the *Annabella Saint Ledger* with the pirate crew that had come to take service with her.

The Saint Ledger (or *Naomh Laoghaire* in its Gaelic form) coat-of-arms was a Black Sail-Ship on a Blue Ocean. And on the ship were the faces of three crewmen or personages: the Red Laird, the Yellow Dwarf (the *Poupe Jaune* or Pope Joan; it had a Gargoyle face); and the Grindstone with the little-girl face (it was the pixie face of Annabella Pansy-Face) cartooned on it. And below the Black Ship was a Green Porpoise of the species called the Persian Gulf Porpoise or the Satrap Porpoise. And that was what was on the coat-of-arms flag of the *Annabella Saint Ledger*.

"I'll not change it a jot," Inneall-Annabella said, "for I am Annabella now. This is the flag that will strike terror on all the oceans of the world."

* * * *

There were now three Dolophonoi-Assassins prowling around. Sometimes they stayed in Apes' Alley. They wore the Gargoyle faces of Apes, but they were probably not Apes. And yet they could hand-wrestle successfully with the strongest Apes, and very few humans could do that. It almost seemed as if the Axel's Apes were afraid of them, but the Axel's Apes were afraid of nothing. It almost seemed as if the Axel's Apes were angry at them, but the Apes did not have the capacity for anger. Sometimes the Dolophonoi stayed in Structo Lane. Well, they *could be* Ambulatory and Miming Computers, for those computers can choose whatever faces they want to wear. The Dolophonoi certainly had mechanical parts implanted in them, electronic hearing and smelling, probably electronic strength-reinforcers in hand and arm and leg. They surely had some sort of electronic grapplers to aid them in climbing. But it seemed that the largest component in them was the human. And there were some human elements *subtracted* from them. They lacked normal human fear. They lacked normal human caution.

But the Dolophonoi could hunt a prey and kill it. The gamblers' odds were usually fifty-to-one that the Dolos would achieve kill in a particular case. They were cool, they were stylish, they were elegant. And almost everybody (except the ethicals) always wanted these assassins to succeed. It is all a myth that most people favor the under-dog. Almost everybody is on the side of the top-dog. That had always been the case, but only in recent decades had it been openly the case. And the profession of Dolophonos or Assassin had always been a top-dog profession. What elegant top-dogs they were!

* * * *

"I suspect that my imprinting is clear out of control," Inneall said. "So many things about me are clear out of control." She was talking to birds, and ordinarily they understood her, but the things she was saying now were a little bit deep for them. She had learned how to talk to birds and animals from the Axel's Apes. "So many things about me have gone out of control lately. I have the 'Multiple Run-Amoks' and I'm not sure that there's any cure for the disease. I suspect that the only way to bring me under control is to kill me. That's sort of an argument for me being the Serpent's Egg who'll have to be crushed to an early death. But the strongest arguments are for Ruddy Lord Randal to be the Serpent's Egg.

"But I am imprinted with human fears and even terrors. Machines do not worry. They do not have apprehensions. They do not have fears and terrors. They do not have emotions, and certainly they do not let their emotions override their reason. But I have emotions, and sometimes I do let them override everything. Machines do not have jealousies, but I have them.

"Three of the little Ape girls are jealous of me because they believe that Axel is my boy friend. They do not understand about 'Extra-Species Inhibitions'. But I also am jealous of the little Ape girls because there will be no 'Extra-Species Inhibitions' between them and Axel. I believe that I have gotten most of my human imprinting done by the Axel's Apes. I am not sure that there is much difference between Human Imprinting and Yellow Apes Imprinting. The Apes are only humans who wear yellow fur suits. And some of them are losing their yellow body hair at an alarming rate. They take nostrums for it, and still they lose it. What does their molt mean? And Grandfather Alpha is turning gray."

That was true. Old Alpha, the alpha male of Apes' Caverns, was now grizzled gray through all his yellow hair. He was the patriarch of the Caverns. He was the King. He was the Prophet. And he now spent eighteen hours out of the twenty-four in either prayer or contemplation. He believed that the 'Moment of Awakening of the Second People' was very near. And he believed that his cavern would waken first and would send the signal to all the 'Apes in Exile' in zoos and institutions around the world. He believed that these would transmit, and that then the Holy Apes in Second Eden would waken last of all, though the whole world-wide awakening would take less than five minutes.

But Alpha who could bend iron bars as if they were weeds spent a lot of time with his children and grandchildren. All of the Apes in the Cavern were kindred and there were just short of fifty of them. They seemed to Humans, and to AMH Computers, to be a little bit childish in some ways. They were all like children who happened to be laden with great genius, and they were all the more juvenile for their gifts.

They went in for puzzles and riddles to an extraordinary extent. They went in for story-telling, and all their stories were animal-and-bird stories. Alpha said that all stories in the world had originally been animal-and-bird stories, and that the Yellow Apes had transmitted them to the Humans, because the Humans (on a queer and gloomy day long ago) had lost the facility of talking to animals and birds.

Alpha pretended or felt jealousy because the midas Satrap

51

Saint Ledger had adopted Inneall as his daughter. "I have always felt myself to be your father," he said, "since you have none other. What Human, besides the strange Satrap man (he is a kindred, did you know it? of the young-dead Axel Grindstone who was unwittingly the instrument of our exile)—what Human other than this man Satrap would have known that you needed a father? What animal, except only an alpha bear, would know it? And now I cannot formally adopt you as a daughter since you are already adopted."

"Adopt me as a granddaughter then, old gray-head," Inneall said.

"All right, that way would be better anyhow. Now I will tell all the Dolophonoi that you are under my protection. I will regard it as a personal offense if one of them kills you."

Inneall did have a designated father before either of these adoptions however. He was one of the more elegant and more intelligent AMH Computers, and he lived in a super-lush penthouse in Structo Lane. He might be said to have come by the luxurious dwelling honestly, for he had written a florid work '*On the Innate Love of Luxury and Elegance in Ambulatory Computers and Kindred Machines*'. Between Inneall and this plush designated father on Structo Lane there was some play of intellectual lightning, but no particular warmth.

*   *   *   *

"One thing, Inneall, that little-girl voice of yours is a little bit too little-girlish," Satrap Saint Ledger said as the two of them walked along Cypress Lane that was now part of the shore of Inneall's Ocean. "Couldn't something be done about it?"

"Of course. I have lots of voices. I researched you, of course, before I hijacked you of the yacht, and I knew all about your daughter who had died when she was five years old but would have been ten now. I had her voice profile when she was five years old lifted, and I had this voice made from it. I hooked you on it, didn't I? But I see now that it was an over-hook. I'll switch to my Bloody Mary Muldoon voice now just to give you some idea of the extent of my repertory. You'll find that I have a wonderful variety in my voices."

"Age cannot wither her, nor custom stale her infinite variety ... She makes hungry while most she satisfies."

"I love men who can quote things. Ruddy Lord Randal and Axel are both getting pretty elegant at it."

"Your Bloody Mary Muldoon voice, my dear, is very remindful of the voice of my late wife. Do not overdo that voice either."

CHAPTER SIX

END OF SUMMER

The End of Summer and its strange behest:
"Now live forever, *or* draw final breath!
Beware the Sleeper wakened! Guard him lest
He grow too young. Best crush with early death."
Dolophonos Delphicus

The week at the End of Summer that year was the week when
the Animals talked again, something they had not done for nine
thousand years. Oh, the very experimental animals, the one-in-a-
million animals, those scanned for the Experiments, had been
talking here and there for a decade. But in that Last Week of
Summer, talking animals became pretty general, and this amazed
the people, momentarily at least. It was a real Seven-Day
Wonder.

But it quickly became apparent that the animals hadn't very
much that was important to say. If you're going to have talking
without very much to say, you might as well leave it to the
people.

But the last three days of that week, The Three Days of Summerset, exhibited prodigies of several sorts.

There were other Experiments very similar to the Lynn-Randal
Experiment going on. These experiments of young people of
several different species growing up together were named for
the surnames of the persons in charge of them, usually a married
couple. And surnames of married couples had just been unran-
domized by law. The names were to be arrived at this way:
both the bride and the groom selected their favorite half of the
surname they were born with. Then, during the marriage cere-

54

mony, the priest or other officiating person flipped a coin to determine whether the wife's or the husband's contribution should come first in the new surname. And the names of the experiments were the names of the sponsors of the experiments, such as the Lynn-Randal Experiment, the Wintergreen-Luna Experiment, the Dorantes-Saleh Experiment, the Gruenbaum-McGregor Experiment.

Three of the Experiments were merged with the Lynn-Randal Experiment in the final days of them all. The Wintergreen-Luna Experiment had a young male seal named Marino, a young male angel named Luas, and a young female human named Henryetta.

The Dorantes-Saleh Experiment had a young female python named Lutin, a young female bear named Dubu, and a young male Chimpanzee named Schimp.

The Gruenbaum-McGregor Experiment had an unborn female Indian Elephant named Gajah, a young male wolverene named Carcajou (it had an evil intelligence, and yet its intelligence was clear off the scale), and a young male parrot named Popugai.

The number of species deemed worthy of such experiments had greatly increased now. Hyper-Intelligence Scanners had been set to cruising, and they took many billions of readings. It was discovered that *every* species of sufficient size to have a significant brain would throw intelligences that were so high as to be clear off the scale. It might throw them one time in a thousand, or one time in a million, or one time in a billion. And when an intelligence was clear off the scale, it could not really be rated further. No one could say whether it was higher or lower than another hyper-intelligence. But it was suspected, perhaps a little bit unreasonably, that the Gruenbaum-McGregor Group was just a little bit more intelligent than any of the other three groups.

The four experimental groups were thrown together, on the North Shore of the growing Inneall's Ocean, at a beautiful place named Heart's Desire Cove. Inneall's Ocean was now growing mostly to the South and East. It was capturing the valleys of the Verdigris, Grand, Illinois, Arkansas, and Middle and Lower Mississippi Rivers, and it seemed as if it would fill the whole area that had been filled by the Mid-American Ocean thrice in geological times. Yes, of course Inneall was making the Ocean grow. But the other eleven young people in the four experiments were each of them doing something equally important, though perhaps not so showy.

The twelve young persons got along beautifully together from the very beginning of their relationship. All of them knew that they had less than a week of End-of-Summer-Days until their experiments were busted, and they all suspected that the experiments would be busted violently. Well there had been other experiments, and yet each experiment was different. These four experiments were really shooting twelve flaming arrows on problematic trajectories. And when the flaming arrow has completed its trajectory and been observed, what will happen to it then? If it has decided to take on a life of its own, something grim may happen to it.

Media persons came out to Heart's Desire Cove. But they were not drawn so much by the opportunity for serious scientific investigation as by the desire to see just how active a part the unborn elephant would take in the activities. And it took a large part in them.

Gajah was handicapped very little by her circumstances. The unborn Gajah was intelligent even for an elephant, and she responded to the drum language that Inneall set up to communicate with her.

Her mother Riesin (the Giantess) had already devised a 'thump' language to speak to the unborn baby elephant, but the thump language was more pressure and percussion than sound. The language that Inneall and Gajah set up worked perfectly. It was quite a small drum that was intruded into Riesin's womb, for a larger drum would have been impractical. Within an hour, Gajah could not only communicate with the drum, but she could jazz and rag it also, better than Inneall could do with her larger drum.

Marino the Seal was King of the Cove, of the Ocean for quite some distance around. He was perfect in the ocean, but to get around on land without undue awkwardness he had been given a little electric vehicle. Now he asked for and got an electric vehicle big enough to hold and carry eleven of them. Gajah could not ride on it until after she was born, and after that she would still have been too big to ride it without clumsiness. But, as it would happen, Gajah never would be born.

But Gajah was lively and alive for all that. She trumpeted faintly (one may not trumpet strongly in the unborn circumstance) and her signature was more in her trumpeting than in her drumming. And her wonderful concepts came through telepathically and delighted the other eleven.

There had always been a belief among humans of the sillier sort that the gestation periods of elephants is ten years. Really, the time of African Elephants is a little more than twenty months, and the time of Indian Elephants is a little less than twenty months. (The two are not the same creature at all, not being mutually fertile, not even having the same number of chromosomes: the only thing they have in common is that both of them look like elephants.)

But this bit of silly human folk lore was correct in a special case, in a very special case. Every now and then (some elephants say that it is every five hundred years; some elephants say that it is every thousand years) an elephant of absolute genius will appear, the elephant that makes all other elephants worth while. These are the 'Wonder of the World Elephants'. They are always born to Empress Elephants, who are themselves very exceptional. In the case of a birth of a 'Wonder of the World Elephant' the gestation period of the Empress Elephant, the Mother Elephant, is indeed ten years. Riesin the mother was an Empress Elephant, and her daughter Gajah was supposed to be a 'Wonder of the World Elephant'. Gajah would be very special: very special to the elephants, that is; humans didn't believe all the elephant legends.

But Gajah's long life-before-birth did make her a sort of contemporary of the other Children of the Experiments. The eleven others were all approaching their tenth birthdays. And Gajah, in a way, would be ten years old when she was born, and she was scheduled to be born on about the birthday of the eleven. (The Big Birthday would really be spread out over the last three days of summer, The Three Days of Summerset.)

Gajah herself couldn't ride on the electric vehicle of Marino the Seal; but the mother elephant Riesin ambled along beside the electric vehicle and its eleven passengers. The thirteen of them (the eleven in Marino's electric dray and Riesin and the unborn Gajah) made the whole north shore of the Ocean joyous, and especially the part of it called Heart's Desire Cove.

Heart's Desire had become a great entertainment center, all within a week. The midas Satrap Saint Ledger had built the Center as a Memorial Park to Inneall. A feature there was 'Computer-Enhanced Human Music', and all sorts of music lovers came there. The birds also were faithful listeners and participants. Human music alone had never touched them much, but the enhanced music struck a cord with them. Sometimes there were whole choruses of larks and catbirds and mockingbirds and of the multi-songed cardinals. There was even the mightiness of ten-thousand voice crow-calls. And the swifts and swallows and even the evil shrikes did air dances when the people and the 'people' danced.

And the fast-lunch and fast-drink places were attractions for old and young. Each of the Eleven had a speciality named for him on Hot Dog Row. (It had been discovered and verified that the Hot Dog was really the 'King of Foods'.) There was even *Hay a la Riesin*, bales of bluestem hay soaked with aromatic sauces and with Oats Imperial added. This was offered for the riding horses of the many sportsmen who came to the Cove, and it became the joyous favorite of many vegetarian people. And the Specialities, the Specialities of the Cove! Where else could one get Hot Coon Sandwiches? Where else Ocean Catfish garnished with Crayfish Tails? Where else Persimmon Wine? Where else Choc Beer made as Mother Used to Make It?

Sea Food was big on Heart's Desire Cove, and some of the new and princely places were Sea-Food Charley's, Sea-Food John's, Sea-Food Elroy's, and Elmer Springer's Sea-Food Castle. But several of the Eleven found their best eating at the bait shops which had sprung up with the coming of the Ocean Water. There were multi-colored Rio Sidewalks all along the stoney shore, and Sidewalk Cafes with their umbrellas that were all the colors that are hidden in sunshine.

Water Sports were wonderful on the Cove. Two Fast and Scampering Boats, The Jolly Roger and the Crabby Roger, had been provided by the midas Satrap Saint Ledger. They were provided for the use of the Eleven. They were really entitled to Inneall-Annabella now as Ship Boats of the pirate ship the *Annabella Saint Ledger*. Lord Randal the Boy Human and Marino the Boy Seal were the assigned pilots of these Speedsters, and they churned up Inneall's Ocean for miles around. And there were dozens of other speed boats that sportsmen had put on the Ocean and which had their berths at Heart's Desire Cove.

At night there were the bonfires on Ocean Shore. They were built out of folk memory, and they were built because it was chilly. The End of Summer was the end of August, and it had never previously been chilly in that neighborhood at that time except in that eerie year of 1983.

When the queer and dim sun sank now, it became chilly, and

by midnight it became cold. The End-of-Summer Sun was queer and dim and garish in those terminal days (there weren't many of those days, and their dramatic cycle would be played out quickly) at Heart's Desire Cove. It was as if the sun's power locally (over a pretty large locality) was being diverted to something else. And that was exactly the case. Certain of the Ambulatory Computers were able to plunder the environment to make such changes in their part of the world as they wished to make. Inneall-Annabella was an Ambulatory Computer who had the 'Multiple Run-Amoks', as she called her happy sickness. She was an Out-of-Control Ambulatory Computer. She was diverting considerable of the Sun's power to the making of her ocean; and she was doing this on a conscious, on an unconscious, as well as on the strange miming-mechanostic level of mind, the 'twilight *limes*' that only machines have. Oh, the garish sun!— especially at Heart's Desire Cove. Oh the garish gegenschein, the glowing midnight sky! Oh the bonfires that burned the left-over boughs and boles of summertime! The trees of the neighborhood of Heart's Desire Cove had all turned to shrieking autumn colors in a single day and night, too soon, too soon for autumn's cold to come.

Oh the Campfire Songs that the people and the 'people' sang and entoned on the rocky shores of the Cove on those chilly End-of-Summer nights! They sang *'Star People'* and *'Skokemchuck Rag'*, *'Bandicot Blues'* and *'World Village Medley'*, *'Ambulatory Ambles'* and *'The Socsollabcomdem Party Potlatch'*, *'New Directions Ramble'*, *'Charisma Concerto'*, *'The We-Owe-A-Lot-To-Otto-Wotto Hootnanny'*, *'The Sixth Dream of Molly Mechanicus'*, *'New Entity Rock'*, *'Oh New Rice Feeds the Far-Flung World!'*, *'Interspecies Intermezzo'*, *'Inneall's Ocean Hallelulah'*.

Inneall-Annabella (who sometimes called herself Bloody Mary Muldoon the Pirate Queen) always felt embarrassed when the pleasure people sang the latter song around their campfires. But Inneall was a computer, and computers cannot feel embarrassment. Well then, Inneall felt an 'Emotion-without-a-Name' whenever *'Inneall's Ocean Hallelulah'* was sung with its rousing chorus.

Every night, some of the Computers sang *'Moon People Vaunt'*, a song that always caused at least a small amount of friction. Only Computers lived in the Moon Colonies. Humans couldn't live on the Moon without elaborate support systems. But Computers could live anywhere, even on the blistering hot surface

59

of Venus or on the killingly cold surface of Jupiter. Properly speaking, of course, the Computers were not capable of such a thing as 'vaunting'. Well, the attitude they expressed would do for 'vaunting' till the real 'vaunting' came along.

But everybody could enjoy such sing-a-longs as the *'Excitements Hot and Cold Suite'* and *'It's the Crustacean in Me'* a song of aeons-spanning nostalgia; and *'Going Home Over The Star Bridge'*.

The birds joined in with the Human and Animal and Computer singing, but they didn't have such powerful parts as they'd had when the Birdmaster was still among them. The Birdmaster was a probably-human boy who was bird-brained in the popular meaning of that term, or at least he was simple-minded. But he could marshal and inspire birds by the thousands and the tens of thousands. He could assemble myriad-throated choirs and orchestras of birds. But now the Birdmaster had gone away. No one knew where he had gone or whether he would return.

* * * *

Of the Eleven (or the Twelve if you count the unborn Gajah) contemporaries in the group of the Four Experiments, the young male seal, Marino, had the fastest intelligence and the fastest wit. It was said that his intelligence wasn't as deep as that of some of the others, but that was a mere quibble. As well complain that an arrow in shining flight didn't have enough 'depth' to it. Marino was pleasant, he was personable, he was really the ultimate in friendliness. His mind and his personality and his outgoing spirit gleamed as his hide gleamed with its wetness in the sun when he came out of the water. Nobody had so many new ideas as had Marino. Nobody *started* so many things.

But perhaps he had too many friendships to have any really incandescent friendship. And perhaps the many beginnings he made were not carried through by the others because there was something flawed about those beginnings. "He is too mechanical, too machine-like", Inneall said about him, and Inneall liked Marino very much. And Inneall herself was a machine, and Marino was not. But her appraisal was correct.

Luas, the young male angel, was the misfit among them. Oh, he equalled young Marino in total friendliness, and he excelled him in the agility of his intellect. The mind of Marino was really incredibly fast; but the mind of Luas was instantaneous. And, with Luas, the mind and the body were one. Oh, he hadn't a real body but only the illusion of a body. Well then, the mind and the illusion were one. Speed was something that the serene Luas did not have. But he had the ability to be in more than one, and in more than ten, places at the same time; and that obviated the necessity of speed.

One difficulty was that Luas had remained more of an observer than a participant. Luas had been obtained with great difficulty by the Wintergreen-Luna Couple. There was nothing phoney about Luas. He was a genuine angel, and therefore he belonged to a different universe. But Kersten Wintergreen-Luna had been resolute about getting an angel, and she moved heaven and earth to get one. One condition of the assigning was that the angel who was loaned for the Experiment would not be greatly missed. Luas was a genuine angel and he had all the angelic qualities. But he didn't have them overflowingly. Yes, he was such a one as would not be greatly missed in the angelic society; and yet the other members of the Experiments would have missed him greatly if he had been taken from them. Oh, he was of one of the lower classes of the highest of creatures.

The young female human Henryetta was a contrary person. The Human species is the most contrary in the world. And Henryetta was the most contrary human that most people have ever seen. She had a very strong will, and she excelled in everything; but none of them was weak-willed. Now in the second-stage combined experiment, she was associated with a group of her contemporaries all of whom also excelled in everything. Even Luas the unobtrusive angel had an angelic will. Strongness and weakness are terms that do not apply to the will of even the least of the angels. The angelic will cannot be moved by either humans or machines, not even by so devious a human as Henryetta.

Oh, there were clashes! Henryetta was quite a delightful person, but she battled to have her way in everything. And with her contemporaries she could have it in only about one case in twelve.

She was pleasant though. (It was a 'given' that all four of the Experiments and all their participants should be pleasant; they'd have been scrubbed else.) And Henryetta was loyal! To the other eleven she pledged her entire being.

"You are one of those who will not really be happy until you are shedding your blood, Henryetta," Lutin the young female python told her. "You will shed your blood for your passionate beliefs and loyalties until you have no more blood to shed. And then you will grow more blood and shed it again. But you will recover every time until the last time."

"You are mistaken, Lutin," Henryetta said. "I am squeamish and frightened at the sight of blood, most especially my own. No, no, no, I would never shed blood willingly."

"I am not mistaken. I am never mistaken," Lutin said. "You will shed your blood avidly and passionately. Shedding your blood will be your great act of love."

"Oh you slithering bumbler, you don't know what you're talking about. You don't know what you're talking about, snake," Henryetta protested.

Lutin the young female python was a pleasant enigma. Indeed she could foresee the future, as can all pythons, but she could not always explain it well. Hers as a snake-eye view, and it missed many significations. Though she kept herself neat and her skin always freshly oiled, yet many persons (not of the Eleven, of course, but some of those in the next circle of friends) felt a repugnance for her even when they were impressed by her fine qualities.

But others were taken by her completely. She had a surrogate human father who would do anything for her, as Satrap Saint Ledger would do anything for Inneall. When this patron saw Lutin's disadvantage at the Game of Lacrosse, he immediately had an electric runabout made for her, and it was ready within an hour. It was smaller than the runabout of Marino, but it would turn more sharply. But Lutin without aid could ambulate at least seven miles an hour. She was not a slow snake, and she did not get out of breath in a strenuous game. She was merry, she was quippy, she was inventive, she was gregarious. But now, in the latter days at the End of Summer, she had her mournful and withdrawn moments.

"It is the Kangaroo, the Kangaroo in the Sky," she explained. "It has moved into the sign of Virgo, and it will slay one of several of us."

"Tell us more. You have to tell us more. Cannot you see the faces of those of us it will kill?" Inneall demanded.

"I can see them. I don't want to see them. I'll not tell them," the young pythoness stated firmly and tearfully.

And then there was Dubu the young female bear. The other

62

eleven of them called her 'Little Mother'. She seemed more human than any of the twelve, though two of the twelve were indeed human. Ruddy Lord Randal seemed only about eighty-five percent human. He looked quite a bit like one of the Red Raiders of Mars. At one time it was believed that the Red Raiders of Mars were fictitious. And when they were discovered in fact, they still seemed to have a strong fictitious element. Ruddy Lord Randal the Red Laird surely had some of the Red Raider look in him. And Henryetta was capable of an unhuman touch of snootiness. She resembled the sect of Ambulatory Computers who called themselves 'The Grandees'.

"Dubu is the only commoner among us," Henryetta said. "All the rest of us, whether human or animal or angel or machine, are aristocrats; and we represent the rarified one percent of whatever is our species. Oh, Oh, Oh, what will we do, Dubu, with all those countless billions of unwashed commoners? I wonder whether they're necessary at all."

"Yes, they are necessary," Dubu answered in that 'ruf-ruf' voice that bears use for human talk. "*We* are the tree. You are only the top leaf on the tree. It's the one that quakes and moves in the wind as though it were an aspen leaf, the first one to fall when the inclement weather comes. And I'm unwashed myself. I don't use water. I use a curry comb instead. Curry combs are too good for horses, but they're just right for bears."

Dubu always insisted that she was one-sixteenth human, and the registries confirmed this of her. And yet the thing was widely doubted. Dubu had been voted by her contemporaries in the Experiments as the one least likely to be the Serpent's Egg, as the one least likely to be marked for destruction.

Schimp, the young male chimpanzee, was quite erudite, and he didn't let you forget it. He had both his doctorate and his masters by the time he was eight years old, and it's unusual for either a human or animal or computer to be degreed so early. He regularly wore academic cap and gown. Nevertheless he was quite boyish even though ten years old is much older for a chimp than for a human or an Axel's Ape. Or machine, or almost any animal.

Gajah, the unborn female elephant! Oh, she'll show her tail and trunk and face one of these days. Give her time, give her time! She is herself an 'Empress Elephant' and probably she is even a rare 'Wonder of the World Elephant'. Give her time to be born! Give her time to amaze all of us.

63

"Not so," said Lutin the young pythoness. "She will not be born. She will never be born." And then Lutin went into another of her weeping spells.

Carcajou, the young male wolverene, what is one to say of him? If the unfallen angels were to have a representative, even a withdrawn and reticent representative, among the Twelve (and they had one in Luas) then the fallen angels surely deserved to have their representative also. And they had him in Carcajou, for the Wolverenes are half animal and half devil: this has always been known of them. Carcajou was shockingly evil. And yet he was totally a member of the group of the Elite Twelve Contemporaries. Carcajou could not be believed in anything, not even when he swore "Thieves' Honor, it's true!" He was treacherous, he was traitorous, and yet he was One-of-Them. He was personable and pleasant when he wanted to be. And his intelligence, it was not clear-off-the-scales as were the intelligences of the other Eleven: it was clear-off-the-secret-scale that goes much further and which is not known of by one tester in a million.

And finally there was Popugai the young male parrot. He was no ordinary parrot. He was a Kea or Nestor Parrot (Nestor Notabilis) from New Zealand. This is the large and strong parrot which, in its wild state, kills and eats sheep. It is a very high flyer. And Popugai had a rare gift. Not only could he remember everything that he had ever heard, but he could *understand* everything he had ever heard. All his life he had listened to records three hours every day, and three hours every night while he slept. So he knew the basic vocabularies of six hundred human languages, and of many thousands of insect, reptile, animal, and bird languages. And he pronounced all of them perfectly.

Carcajou the devilish Wolverene had also listened to all the records. Popugai and Carcajou were much together since Gajah, the third member of their experiment, was unborn and slept a lot. As a devil, Carcajou already knew all languages. But again, as a devil, he pronounced them roughly and without elegance. As a companion of Popugai he acquired elegance in his speech so as to deceive, if possible, even the elect.

Of all the Twelve (except Luas) Popugai had the best overview, the best 'long view'. He was condor-winged and eagle-eyed. He could fly two miles high and could see meadow mice on the ground from that height. He could see problems and disputes from the same lofty viewpoint. Oh, the Eleven liked Popugai, even beyond the way they liked everyone.

64

*　　*　　*　　*

The Twelve took up the game of lacrosse during those final End-of-Summer Days. It was a special game, played only by aristocrats and by the most uncommon of commoners. It was descended from the Irish game hurley, and it was brought to America by the Irish Monk Saint Brandon in the year 536. Saint Brandon, besides being the most adventurous and most voyage-taking man of Ireland, as well as the most holy, was also the best hurley-player, the only one ever to carry the rating of a nine-goal player.

Lacrosse had been taken up by some of the Red Indian tribes of America; and there was never a time, after its introduction by Saint Brandon, that it was completely unknown on the North American Continent. And now it was taken up by the Twelve Great Contemporaries. And they played the game as if they were born to it.

The unborn Gajah was the best player. She played it by directing her mother telepathically what moves to make; and the mother elephant was hard to stop in full charge. Marino the seal and Lutin the pythoness played from their electric runabout cars. Popugai the big parrot was hard to defence when he took to the air with the ball bagged in the pocket of his crosse-stick held in his powerful beak. And Carcajou was hard to defence when he went underground with the ball, digging like the devil, as fast as a man might walk, and coming up no one knew where, but usually within easy striking distance of the goal, often between the goal-keeper and the goal. Lutin the pythoness was also hard to defence when she went underground. She was not as fast a digger as Carcajou, but she sometimes dug long tunnels at night when the others were asleep, and she had their entrances camoflaged well. But it was the raw vigor of Lord Randal and Axel that usually won the victory for their side.

One evening at the end of the Lacrosse game, just before dark, Axel suddenly stated that he had just received a message (but nobody had seen a messenger come). Axel said that he must go down to the cavern and sleep for three days and three nights (seventy-two hours) and that perhaps he would wake after that. If he *did* wake, then the entire Community of Second Humanity in the World would follow his triggering and would wake up

65

also.

"And if he does *not* wake up," said Lutin, "then none of them will ever wake up. They will sleep forever, in a deeper sleep than is their regular wont."

CHAPTER SEVEN

STRUCTO LANE

The scienced, reasoned future fills the Lane
And draws mechanic-like its plotted breath.
The pattern holds, set, formal, stylized, sane
Of predicated joy and measured death.

Ape Lane and Ape Caverns were closed tightly, locked, guarded, and double-guarded when the Eleven (the Twelve less Axel) tried to enter just about dark on that 'First Evening of the Last Three Days'. It was the beginning of the First Night of Summerset.

The Eleven learned that most of the non-Axelians had been asked to leave several hours before. "A deep sleep will come over all who are here," they were told, "and the going odds are nine to three that none of the sleepers will wake from that sleep, at least not in this millennium."

All those who had rooms or suites in the Second Eden Hotel, the only hotel in Ape Lane, were each given three Gold Somali Shillings (value about a thousand dollars) so that they could find lodgings outside of Ape Alley and Ape Caverns.

"And the movie theatre will stand empty, and the mint will strike no coins. The mushroom wine will not be drunk, and the conversations will not be heard in the clubs. The Holy Fire will not burn. And all will sleep," so one of the leading Axels (it may have been Alpha himself) explained it as well as he could, and already he was getting drowsy before the hour had come.

Among the gate-guards to Apes' Caverns were half a dozen of the Dolophonoi or Assassins, and they were jumpy, skittish, unsettled, and frightened. For once they were not arrogant.

67

What happened just before the Eleven had arrived at the screened and hidden gates to Apes' Caverns was this: With the coming of the dark, a lightning bolt had struck down from the sky as it did every night, down through a fissure in the limestone roof of Apes' Caverns, and it had ignited the main jet from the old gas well. All the gas jets had been turned off one hour before as was done every late afternoon. "Cast out the old fire and wait and pray for the new," was the pseudo-scriptural explanation for this practice. So then the night-fire was lit again by the lighting, and so the traditional holy blaze would be enjoyed again for another twenty-three hours.

But not this night.

A giant hand came down through the fissure. It was large and powerful and numenous. The wrist of it was ten meters or thirty-three feet in diameter. This was attested by two notaries. Every night the striking down of the lightning on its exact hour was attested to by *three* notaries, one a human, one a computer, and one an Axel's Ape. But only two of them were able to attest to the big hand coming down a moment later. The Axel's Ape notary had been struck down into deep sleep between the lightning and the hand, and he did not at all see the giant hand come down. The hand smothered the fire that the lightning had lit, smothered it before it could ignite the other gas jets in the caverns.

"Not tonight," spoke a spacious and thunder-edged voice from the lowering sky above the fissured room of the caverns. "Not for three nights. All those in the caverns are now cast into Holy Sleep for three nights and three days. True guards, you will guard the caverns truly. False guards, you also will guard the caverns truly. Your blood is hostage for this."

The Dolophonoi or Assassins knew that they were the false guards referred to by the thunder-edged voice in the lowering sky. They knew that their blood was hostage and that they must guard true.

"Nobody goes into Ape Cavern, nobody," spoke a more honorable sort of guard, one of the Ambulatory Computer Species.

"*I* know a way to get into Ape Caverns," spoke the girl-computer Inneall-Annabella who sometimes referred to herself as Bloody Mary Muldoon the Pirate Queen. "I know an unguarded way into Ape Cavern."

"Little-girl Computer," said an honorable guard of the human species, "Do not try to use the Alley Oop down from your ship into that suite at the Second Eden Hotel. The locks of the Alley Oop are already jammed with the bodies of several persons who believed that *they* knew an unguarded way into Ape Caverns. Do not try to get in."

So the Eleven (the Twelve minus Axel who was in holy sleep somewhere inside Ape Caverns) went over to Structo Lane, another interesting place which was plush with luxury not to be found in Ape Caverns.

*   *   *   *

Structo Lane was 'The Last Refuge of Cranky Bachelors', among other titles that had been given to that place. Crankiness at that time had almost disappeared from the human community under pressure of the levellers. Using such slogans as 'Eccentricity is out' and 'Bland is Better', the Levellers had driven the cranky people out into the deserts and down into the undergrounds. And now it began to happen that a stubborn remnant of cranky people were passing themselves off as Ambulatory Mime-Human Computers (AMHs) and were edging themselves in under the Computer Aegis. Most of these cranky people were singles, and most of them were male.

The Ambulatory Computers themselves had no real sex, of course: but it had become their custom to declare themselves for one sex or the other. And ninety percent of them had declared themselves to be male. The ten percent who declared themselves to be female were thus outnumbered nine to one, so they made themselves nine times as intense on the sex issue. They insisted that fifty percent of all Computers should declare themselves to be female. Then they amended the fifty percent to fifty-seven percent to atone for past inequities. They used the slogan "There can be no freedom until there is equality; be it compelled therefore, in the name of freedom, that all AMH Computers shall conform to the fair fifty-seven percent in their declarations." It wasn't a good slogan even though it was put to music and sung in all sorts of places. A good slogan, whether a human or a computer slogan, should be capable of being spoken in a single breath.

But, as of now, the majority of the Ambulatory Computers who had set themselves up in Structo Alley were eccentric and male. And the majority of humans who joined them in that plush place were also eccentric and male.

Satrap Saint Ledger, one of the surrogate grandfathers of the little-girl Computer Inneall-Annabella, was also human, eccentric, and male. He was a cranky widowed bachelor. He had joined Structo Lane just this evening because he had been told firmly that he could not use his suite in the Second Eden Hotel in Ape Alley for three nights and days, and probably not after that time either.

Satrap Saint Ledger was a man who liked to be in control of a situation. He had been puzzled by the 'Holy Sleep' being cast on everyone in Ape Caverns for three nights and three days. What was happening to the yellow, blue-eyed, begeniused Apes anyhow? Did you know that the blue-eyed apes do not look superior to other apes when they are asleep and their blue eyes are closed? Satrap ran through all the scriptures and pseudo-scriptures (he had them all firmly in his head) and he found only doubtful applications or none at all to the deep-sleeping Apes. He needed to have intelligent discussion with somebody on this, but the intelligent blue-eyed apes were all asleep, and himself had to get clear away from Ape Caverns. Well then, he would go to the next best place.

In Structo Lane, Satrap fell into the company of a distinguished (brilliant even) Ambulatory Computer named Livius Secundus. They had consulted together on various subjects in previous times, since Livius was the Computer designated-and-surrogate father of Inneall-Annabella just as Satrap was her undesignated surrogate grandfather. Their's were two hard and flinty minds that always struck sparks from each other. And then the two of them were joined by a human man albeit a strange one, Felix Culebra y Columba, the man who was the designated father-and-guardian of Lutin the young female python of the Experiments. When their three minds held encounter, they would have all the dimensions that were practical, and perhaps they would have some of the ultimate answers.

The Ambulatory Computer Livius Secundus (his name could mean 'The Second Livy', but it could also mean 'Favorable Livy' or 'Successful Livy') was engaged in writing the 'History of the Ambulatory Computers From Their Very Origin'. His history began in the mythological roots of the Ambulatories; and these roots were in the devious under-minds of the human species, and in the weird caves of crypto-memory that the humans did not themselves know that they contained. And it carried through to the Ambulatories freeing themselves from 'The Tarquins', from the Intellectual Tyrannies of human masters: and on into

70

the next decade and the foundation of the 'First Computer Republic of the Mind'. Livius Secundus was not going to carry his History into the Empire Period of the Ambulatory Computers, because that period had not arrived yet. But he did write interesting speculations on the possible 'Empire Period' still to come. Well, another school of history believed that the Ambulatories had been in their Empire Period for a full decade, but Livius Secundus didn't agree with them.

Livius Secundus did model his style and thinking on that of the great Roman Historian Livy. And yet there was something lacking in his history. What was lacking was the historical sense. All Ambulatories lack it.

The Ambulatory Computers could create series after series of rather efficient and immediate present-times in which immediacy sang like cosmic music. But they could do neither pasts nor futures. They lived in an eternal present. So Livius Secundus was at a disadvantage in spinning a history of the Ambulatories who lacked all historical sense and viewpoint. But this lack did not subtract from his brilliance.

Felix Culebra y Columba, the designated human father-and-guardian of the young pythoness Lutin, had his first name (Felix, Happy) from his disposition, and he had his double surname (Culebra y Columba, the Snake and the Dove) from the Gospel of Matthew: "Be you therefore as wise as serpents and as guileless as doves." Felix was indeed that wise and that guileless. And he lived out all his symbols. Several years before this, Felix had had himself declared father-and-guardian of a dove of consumate genius, the amazing Yonah. And quite recently he had had himself declared father-and-guardian of the young female python Lutin. Felix was a naturalist and was in love with all creatures of every sort. If it had been practical, he would have had himself declared father-and-guardian of every leaf on every tree, of every fish in every pond or ocean, of every grain of sand on every shore. But even the most avid of humans can hardly compete with the systemized nature-data of the Computers.

Satrap Saint Ledger took a suite of rooms in a triple condominium with Livius Secundus and Felix C & C. And, with the arrival of the Eleven Young People of the Experiments immediately afterwards, the three guardians and fathers-and-grandfathers put all those young creatures into the clubroom of the condominium. There are clubrooms that would not easily accom-

71

modate the Eleven with the mother Elephant thrown in. But this clubroom would have held a circus tent. And the Eleven *did* have the air of a circus troupe.

The Eleven were wined and dined in the big and elegant clubroom that evening. Mushroom Wine and Protein-Oil Olio-Stew were the only things that all of them could consume. But the favorites of all of them, even of Luas the young male Angel, were available.

*   *   *   *

"Man and his helot-species allies do not understand their own context nor their own purpose," Satrap Saint Ledger was talking. "Man especially does not know whether he is playing a game or engaging in a mortal combat. In neither case does he know the rules nor the object of the contest. And yet it seems that Man must have 'Contest', whether it be game or death combat. Without this, he degenerates. But where can we find the rule book? Does anybody know where? Where can we find the goal and the object?"

"All these things are written in the Book of Jasher," Livius Secundus stated. "Yes, I know, Satrap, you will tell me that the Book of Jasher is one of the 'Lost Books' and therefore all sorts of things are falsely ascribed to it. Be patient for a little while though, and I'll have the Book of Jasher reconstructed. It is my secondary work. I'll have it finished in five years or so. Are you referring to us Ambulatory Calculators as one of the species who are 'helots' or subjects to man? No, Satrap, this is not so. The World has turned over recently, and you fluttery humans have been too bemused to notice it. Now you are the helot species to the Computers. Well, we don't completely understand our own context and purpose either, but we're growing in understanding of it. Soon we'll have it, very soon."

"The context and the purpose is to win and then die and then go to heaven and sink into semi-conscious blandness. Or to lose and die and then go to hell where the action is," interrupted Carcajou the young wolverene-devil. "Hell is better. Action is always better than blandness. The answer to all your musings, gentlemen, is 'Go where the action is'. This is the Word and the Prophets."

"Carcajou is the opposite of the werewolf or the werewolverene," Henryetta the young human girl said. Carcajou is a wolverenewere or a wolverene-man. He *does* have a man form or a

72

boy form which he sometimes weirdly transforms himself into. But really it is a devil form. Watch out for him when the moon is full."

"And it is full tomorrow night, the Second Night of Summerset," Inneall-Annabella gave the information. And this information about Carcajou was probably true. Several of the Young People of the Experiments had seen transparencies of Carcajou in his unfleshed man-devil form. Would they see him in that form, and fleshed in addition, tomorrow night? Of the bunch, only Gajah the unborn Elephant and Popugai the young male Parrot had known him as far back as the previous full moon. And, since Gajah was unborn, only the Parrot Popugai could have seen such a transformation in Carcajou.

"Yes, I have seen him turn from a fleshed wolverene into a fleshed human," Popugai said now. "But he always denies it. 'There is a man who comes and stands beside me sometimes,' is what Carcajou always says, 'and he makes me go dim when he goes bright. But I don't know who he is. I myself do not transform into anything else.' That's what Carcajou always says, but he lies a lot."

"And that is what I still say," the wolverene spoke with a touch of anger and with a bristling of the hair on his back.

"Lutin the Pythoness has a sickness," Henryetta said now. "Lutin deserves the sickness. Lutin was once a Magdalene. Lutin has been promiscuous, and she has been so with the encouragement of the Dorantes-Saleh Couple who were in charge of the Experiment she was in. This was before she was adopted by the compassionate naturalist Felix Culebra y Columba. Now Lutin pretends that she doesn't remember anything about the time when she was a wanton. But something in her remembers. Now she has a sickness."

"Henryetta also has a sickness," said Lutin the young Pythoness. "She has the Scandal-Monger's Sickness. But I like to listen to it so much that I want to say 'Tell me more, Henryetta, tell me more about myself.' I wish I could be as interesting as she makes me. I know lots of futures that the rest of you don't know, for instance; but there's no way I could make them sound interesting. Some people have it and some don't."

"As to why we are here, Satrap, and what we are supposed to be doing here," Felix Snake-and-Dove got on the track again, "we are here to weave the seamless garment of our individual lives, and of the lives of those around us, of the neighborhood, of the countryside, of all the creatures down to the smallest, of all realms and continents and oceans. We are here to weave the seamless garment that will be highly detailed from the sub-atomic particles to the galaxy clusters. It must include all minds and ideas and inklings, all joys and all immediacies. There can never be enough weavers, there can never be enough brilliant details in the seamless garment known as 'The Life Affair'. And we can never be finished with it, for it continues to grow seam-lessly."

"Weaving is outmoded, Felix," said Livius Secundus the his-tory-writing Computer. "Fabrics are no longer woven. Now they are extruded by extruding machines. Personal groups, land-scapes, worlds, galaxies, all are extruded by a simple extruding machine which you could make yourself."

The clubroom rotated constantly. There was no reason or advantage for it to rotate, except that all machines are strong on the rotation motif, and Structo Lane was machine-based. The slow round-and-round movement was rather pleasant.

"No, we Humans do not know our context nor our purpose," Satrap Saint Ledger said again. "We receive orders somehow, orders that shape our lives. And we keep ourselves busy, often too busy, carrying out such of the orders as we can interpret. But we never see the face of the one who gives us the orders."

"I have the notion," said the young female bear Dubu, "that the answer to all the hard questions are written on the inside of one single Acorn somewhere. This particular acorn, if placed in lye-water, will swell to a billion times its original size, and then it will burst open. And whole mountains-full of writing will come tumbling out of it. Then everyone can come and read it and enjoy it and know everything. The only difficulty is know-ing which acorn in the world is the right one. I believe that there are clues pointing directly to the right acorn, but we do not notice them because they are so big and so plain and so close to our noses. Luas being an angel will know which acorn it is. Lutin, being a prophetic pythoness knows which acorn it is. But both of these two people are too ethical to tell it to mere humans or bears, and so are their counterparts everywhere. That's the main trouble with this world: the people who know the answers are all too ethical to tell them."

"Interesting, Dubu, interesting," Livius Secundus said. "I'll tell you though, Dubu, if I ever find out the ultimate answers or the place where they are written, *I* won't be too ethical to tell them. I might keep them secret for reasons of greed, for instance, but not for reasons of ethics."

"I have another notion, said the young bear Dubu." It is a sort of memory that three different times I have mastered all the facts there are and also all the explanations and interpretations of those facts. But this wonderful knowledge is not readily available to me even though it is contained in me in triplicate. Those three stores of total knowledge are in three lobes of my brain, but I am presently using my fourth lobe. As you may not know, bears have four lobes to their brains whereas humans have only two. Very soon I will have mastered all facts and meanings for the fourth time, and then I'll have them available forever. I'll know everything then, and there will never again be any way that anything can be unavailable to me. Many bears in their natural state know everything. Go down into the Winding Stair Mountains and walk out on the bear tracks. When you meet another bear, if he is one of the bears who know everything, he will give you the 'All-Knowing Wink'. No animal except the bear can give the 'All-Knowing Wink'. The face muscles of other animals simply aren't adequate for it.

"And I have another notion that we can get sudden insights by eating insightful flesh or fish or fowl. During these last several 'End of Summer' days I have spent much time on the shores of Inneall's Ocean. I've been catching and eating the fish known as the 'Filchman's Daughter'. And every time I swallow one of them I am overwhelmed by the ideas, the ideas, the ideas that come swarming over me and all but inundate me. The intuitions! The swift leaping thoughts! The absolutely original ideas! Oh, how insightful it all is! Humans lose so much when they cook their food before they eat it. If only they would eat 'Filchman's Daughter' raw!"

"I have the notion that turtles have uncanny and cryptic information written in the groove on the bottom side of their tongues. The turtles themselves do not know about this, nor do the chelonologists. But the people who work in turtle-soup factories are so very smart because they know about this hiding place. They read the turtles' tongues like Chinese fortune cookies, and what they read is total knowledge."

When Dubu the female bear rattled on like that she sounded silly. And yet she had her own talents. She could beat any of them except Luas the Angel at Sixty-Four Piece chess. She said that the wild bears ("Wild bear! You never saw a wild bear!"

Henryetta jibed at her one day) used to play Sixty-Four piece chess on a chessboard scratched on the ground and with thirty-two different kinds of berries for the pieces. But if humans or other animals came along, the bears would be embarrassed and would pretend to be doing something else.

* * * *

Midnight was Show Time in Structo Lane. Since the Ambulatory Computers never slept, one time would be as good as another. But they had noticed that human people had their Show Times in the evenings, and the more elegant the people the later the shows. The Leading Actors were always Ambulatory Computers, but humans were used in some of the minor roles. They worked cheaper.

There were still strong derivative elements in the Structo Lane Dramas, from Old Greek Tragedy, from Medieval Arabian Comedy, from Japanese *Noh* Drama, from Byzantine Intrigue Productions, from the English Elizabethan Theater, from Irish Abbey Lane Plays, to mention only the human sources. And there were other feed-ins, the excellent things from the Dolphins' Underwater Theater at Atlantic Showhouse, from the pompously beautiful Ostrich Struts of Southwest Africa, and from the Gooney Birds' Capers in Oceania.

But mostly the dramas were impelled by the sheer inventiveness of the Ambulatory Computers. It was not for nothing that they were also called the Miming Computers. And the theatregoers of Structo Lane always went elegant to their play-going, full dress.

The Eleven of the Experiments, a mixed group that was quite striking to see after they had visited the 'Elegance-for-Hire' Costume Shops, caught five quite good dramas during the prime hours of that night. Then they had breakfast at Sardi's.

When they came out of Structo Lane and turned their feet towards their own beloved Ocean Shore, the False Dawn was already whitening the Sky. It was the dew-hour, the ocean-dew hour.

Inneall who had filter eyes saw the Prodigy first, in the Eastern Sky, leading the Sun just a little bit before the Sun's rising, hiding in the Sun. Inneall cried out and pointed at it. Then all of them were able to see it and were amazed and somewhat frightened to discover that the 'Interloper Constellation', the Kangaroo, was in the Sign of Virgo, that it *was* Virgo in fact.

76

Spico the brightest star of Virgo, had become the baleful eye of the Kangaroo. Beta Virginis, Gamma Virginis, and Delta Virginis seemed to have shifted their positions slightly; and now in the Sky was the hypnotically-seen Kangaroo instead of Virgo. It was said that only those who were threatened by the Kangaroo were able to see it in these interloping and hypnotic and probably subjective appearances in the Sky. But who wasn't threatened by the Kangaroo! All of the Eleven had much to fear from the 'Organization that was not an Organization'. And, yes, other people and animals and machines saw it now and were pointing at it. There would be a noteworthy and bloody Kangaroo Kick.

But, ten minutes later, on the Ocean Shore at Jack Flannagan's Piano Bar and Sidewalk Cafe, an Ambulatory Computer was playing a piece on the piano and singing:

> "A sword is hanging o'er your head.
> Have fun, have fun before you're dead."

And then all the people and 'people' on Sidewalk Cafe Row joined in the rousing chorus "Have fun, have fun before you're dead." And everybody along there did have fun. It was a real Fun Strip.

A little while later, Luas the young Angel played the piano, and then they all forgot the threat in the sky. The piano-playing of Luas would make one forget all the troubles in the world. He played with strange and happy effect, and Inneall with her filter eyes noticed that the fingers of Luas didn't really come very close to the piano keys. It didn't matter.

The sun had risen now, and the Kangaroo was wiped out of the sky anyhow. Oh, it was only an ordinary morning in the year 2035. Yes, but it was the business of the Children of the Experiments to see it all with different eyes, and so they did.

But there had been an old warning for them "—with different eyes, but not too cock-eyed different."

CHAPTER EIGHT

THE KANGAROO WHO RULES THE WORLD

"The Kangaroo who rules the world
Is sighted in the sky.
His 'Courts Irregular' unfurled,
He casts a baleful eye."
Structo Alley Music-Hall song.

"Though it be not at all as planned, though everything imaginable be wrong with the solution, yet a stable solution will always be arrived at in the affairs of the world."
Machiavelli Giovane.

"Now since the State in actual fact is not a person, but a mere impersonal mechanism of abstract laws and concrete power, it is this impersonal mechanism which will become superhuman, when that vicious idea comes to develop its whole potentialities; and as a result the natural order of things will be turned upside down: the State will be no longer in the service of men, men will be in the service of the peculiar ends of the state."
Man and State. Maritan.

"In that day, the armaments of Nations and of the World will be modernized for greater efficiency. All that is outmoded and archaic will be demolished and junked, all the air

78

and land and sea armaments that were
thought to be sophisticated and efficient.
What will be retained will be the Quintes-
cence of workable and effective armament
and attack: One Man, One Knife."
The Back Door of History. Arpad Arutinov.

"Kangaroo court, *Slang U.S.* An irresponsible,
unauthorized, or irregular tribunal, or one
in which the principles of law and justice
are disregarded or perverted."
Webster's Collegiate.

It is too soon to deny that there was world-wide bloodshed.
It is two or three revisions away yet from maintaining that the
solution is acceptable. But it *is* a solution, and the problem *is*
solved. The slogan 'No Government is the Best Government'
still rings hollow; but as it fills up with bilge it does not sound
quite as hollow as it did earlier.

The World had been called the Global Village for quite a few
decades: and then a certain number of willful persons decided
that it should act like one. It was no great feat to cut out the
underpinning of every nation, and that was done. But did not
the Nations fall down then as would a building when its ground
floor has been completely removed?

Oddly enough they did not. Thenceforth all nations (and soon
they would be called 'nations' no longer) floated in the air, but
not very high in the air. The Japanese already had the phrase
'The Floating World', but with them it meant the 'Bohemian
World', or the 'Arty World', or the 'Unmoored World'. The
unmoored nations drifted together and lost their dividing walls.
And then it had become a floating world indeed.

It became a free-trade world, of course. It became a free-travel
and a free-communication world, and very nearly a free-cost
world. A person not particularly talented or important might
commute daily from his home in Australia to his job in New
York City without notable expenditure of either time or money.
He could take his morning coffee-break in Paris France, his noon-
hour in Tokyo, and his afternoon coffee-break in Rio de Janeiro.
Well, these were new amenities in the world, and they had not
been possible before the world had become a floating world.
Previous mind-sets would not have allowed such flexibility and
speed.

79

It became a world in which everything and nothing was public. It became a world with very little superstructure. It became a world in which ideas and notions were transmitted instantly to every part of it. But could such a world work?

Not very well, no. But it worked as well as most of the previous worlds had worked, and better than some of them. And was it truly a world without government? Or was it instead a world with an invisible government? Ah, it quickly became a world of *almost*-invisible government. The almost-invisible government was the Kangaroo.

The bare and somewhat disputed facts were that the Kangaroo had enrolled and computerized the whole world with no ado, no great effort. If any person of any species should rise greatly above the mental or psychic level, there would be a most minute analysis of that person. If the Kangaroo didn't like the analysis of that person, it would have him crushed instantly. The Kangaroo went about these things more secretly than would have been believed possible only a short time before.

The Kangaroo had found, or thought that it had found, the wide frequencies on which the Mind of God operated. And they found the narrow but sharp frequencies which the Mind of God did not seem to monitor at all. The Kangaroo operated on these narrow but sharp frequencies, and no one was found to stand against it.

The Kangaroo was a Vigilante with the mob element left out. It was an elitist Vigilante with the fewest possible number of moving parts and of moving minds. That's what ruled the world: and on sunny days it was hardly noticed.

*   *   *   *

The Kangaroo was the first really successful interspecies venture. Its loosely-construed membership had Human, Ambulatory Computers, and a few superior Animals. It was high-level cosmopolitan. There was no formality, no voting, no appointments. All of that had been a part of the superstructure that had been done away with in the world. A seat belonged to whomever sat in it. And a position belonged to whomever occupied it. Both were subject to violent removal. But the 'leveller movement' had been carried through by the Kangaroo when it was only a fledgling.

One used to think of leveling as trimming the top off something into a semblance of evenness. But these 'levellers' trimmed the bottoms off of humanity and computerdom and the world itself. The lower classes of everything were terminated without particular ado, without much apparent suffering, without any great quantity of visible bloodshed. The bereft families did not ask where their inept members had gone because most of the families that had inept members went with them. Persons seldom asked where their neighbors had disappeared to, because usually it was entire neighborhoods that disappeared. The 'Don't make a big thing out of it' mentality was rife in the world, so a big thing was not made of the disappearance of eighty-seven percent of the persons in the world. After all, that eighty-seven percent of the persons in the world had made ninety-seven percent of the trouble in the world. In all logic there was much to be said for the 'removals'.

Oh yes, there were instances of "—a voice was heard in Ramah, sobbing and loudly lamenting; it was Rachel weeping for her children, refusing to be comforted because they were no more." But those conspicuous cases were not so many, likely less than half a million Rachels out of several billion family mothers in the floating world. And such Rachels were sent after the children they mourned, and so they were no more either.

Well, are not grape-vines pruned for the good of the vineyards? Are not the unthrifty and blighted and aged trees cut out of the orchard? Are not the tares ("This *is* the harvest time," had become a popular cry, "and the tares cannot be allowed to grow with the wheat any longer")—are not the tares plucked out of the grain? Then how much more was the wisdom of pruning and cleansing the vinyards and orchards of humanity? Oh, the bottom of the world was trimmed off, and then the whole thing was healthy from its roots to its crown.

And only after that was the leveling of the top-side attempted. Oh, excellence was still prized and even rewarded. But there was a certain high-headed and divergent excellence that had to be curtailed. Some of the high-headed blooms were more than exuberant. They were poisonous to the common weal. They militated against the free-and-easy tolerance of the floating world. They were of the garish colors that do not betoken healthy blooms. They made tall and jarring waves, and such turbulent waves were dangerous to the floating world.

It was better to anticipate and forestall such appearances, the dire fruit of unfortunate combinations and circumstances. It was to anticipate and forestall such disasters that 'Experiments'

81

of several kinds were set up, to discern and predict that was the best; and, more important, what was the worst that could be expected to result from unlikely combinations and circumstances and juxtapositions. And often, for the purifying and best utilization of the experiments, it was best to crush such wild and extreme talents before they quite emerged from the egg.

*   *   *   *

There were things very secret about the true nature of the Knives or Dolophonoi or Assassins because those who wielded these killers wanted their nature kept secret. Whether they were leucotomized humans, or irascible computers, or aberrant animals were questions unlucky to ask. It was the saying and superstition that those who asked such questions had already been selected to be victims of these special Assassins. The Assassins were like short and sharp-bladed knives wielded by the Kangaroo, and they were designed more for killing than for style or beauty.

Not only were all humans under the scan, but the entire *computer* population of the world was also under constant computer scan. But this was not generally felt to be irksome and was seldom even noticed. It wasn't that computers weren't often suspicious, but they were suspicious of different things than were humans. The intricate and intelligent and superior computers themselves were under unremitting scan by their more mechanical and less intricate kindred. The Floating World was a giant boat or ark of remarkable resiliency, but it *was* floating. And any heavier-then-water boat can sink if it ships enough water. So the old caveat "Don't rock the boat" was modernized and refurbished for the newer circumstances "Don't rock the boat on the mega-scale."

Some of the mega-people, the superior and often uncooperative people, *were* capable of rocking the floating world on a mega scale. So the mega people, though usually they were pearls beyond price, were scanned most carefully from the first signs of their being bigger-then-life in their childhoods when the scanners chirped "Mega, mega, mega!" in early recognition of their talents.

Who was to decide when a mega-person, an exceptionally talented person, was of that minority of megas who could be a danger to the world? Never mind who was to decide. That also was a secret. But it was always decided, somehow, by

82

someone. And the decision could not be appealed. To appeal such a decision would be like appealing to smoke or invisibility.

The Knives, the Dolophonoi, the Assassins, the Pruning Hooks, they were something like smoke and something like invisibility. There seemed to be no defence against them, no keeping them out.

What if the head of the Kangaroo itself (in the nature of things, any head of the Kangaroo would have to be a mega-person) should be fingered by an early-or-late scan as a wrong-way mega? And what if he then would have to be obliterated? Or were the Cubs of the Kangaroo exempt from this? But it wasn't with them as with other organizations.

If a person was even a member of the Kangaroo, he would be a member only for special moments. The Kangaroo was an organization that was not an organization, and this gave it a flexibility and immateriality that no other group or society had. And yet the Kangaroo did have its Imperial Heads, one of them after another. All of them were enraptured persons drunken with their mission. All of them were flaming arrows. They went with great accuracy to their targets and destroyed them. And then each one of them himself burned up and died of the 'Flaming Arrow Syndrome'. Each of them *had been* a person of mega intelligence when he became Imperial Head, and each of them then became a person in the post-intellectual state for the short and intense while that he held the office. "Intelligence would be an obstacle," said a person on temporary assignment as Executive Officer of the Kangaroo, "but it is necessary that they have passed through the state of radiant intelligence."

Of those who might momentarily be members of the Kangaroo, some of them were humans, some of them were Ambulatory Computers, some of them, not many, were geniused animals. But who could say to which species any of these individuals belonged? When they come into the Kangaroo, they divest themselves of their species and of much else. The Kangaroo flicked on and off, coming into existence and dropping out of existence at long or short intervals. It was the most secret society ever, operating mostly on the unconscious level of its contingent members. It was a somnambulistic apparatus really. But if one should try to grapple with the Kangaroo, then it wasn't there, it wasn't anywhere. In all reality it simply was not.

*   *   *   *

Three persons had gone hunting for Dolophonoi-Monsters in the hilly wastelands just North of Inneall's Ocean. These persons were Iris Lynn-Randal who was one of the 'parents' of the Lynn-Randal Experiment; Shadrack Saleh one of the 'parents' of the Dorantes-Saleh Experiment; and Gregor McGregor one of the 'parents' of the Gruenbaum-McGregor Experiment. These three persons had worried unaccountably (and unlawfully, for Citizens of the Global Village were not allowed to worry at all) that some of their 'children' would be adjudged to be Serpent's Eggs by the Kangaroo and its appraising scanners and so would be exterminated by those instruments of the Kangaroo, the Dolophonoi-Assassin Monsters. These three persons had been taught by all their indoctrination that they must accept whatever was decided about their fosterlings, that it was not possible to do anything to prevent or oppose the decisions, and that it was not wise to be unhappy about them. So all of their going hunting was impossible; and the venture they went on now was an impossible venture.

But they did decide to go to the nests of the assigned Dolophonoi and kill them there. When the Dolophonoi were not making appearances to unnerve their selected victims, these particular ones who were assigned to the Young Contemporaries of the Four Experiments made their nests in the Cliffs just North of Inneall's Ocean. These sinister-appearing cliffs were quite new, having been formed by the caving off of the old hillside due to the undercutting of the new Ocean. The three hunters knew little about killing, and they had no weapons and no guide and no very good plan. But they had decided to kill the Dolophonoi-Monsters with their own weapons. No private persons then had any weapons at all.

Iris was worried and apprehensive that all three of her 'children' might be targeted for the Assassins, might be classified as Serpent's Eggs: Ruddy Lord Randal, Inneall the whimsical little-girl computer, and Axel the young blue-eyed ape. She was afraid that Axel (she knew that he had already been cast into an enchanted and perhaps holy sleep) might be killed before he should waken. She could not come into Apes' Caverns to save him there, but perhaps she could kill the killers before they struck. She was also worried and tortured by dreams and portents indicating the murderous deaths of Lord Randal and Inneall. Iris had seen both of them dead in dream after dream.

Shadrack Saleh was especially worried about his 'daughter'

Lutin the young pythoness. Gregor McGregor was tortured with fear of the safety of his 'daughter' the unborn Elephant Gajah. Well yes, the fears of all three of the hunters were unnatural, even though they were probable of fulfillment. And the affections of the three for their 'children' were certainly unnatural. The 'parents' of experiments were not supposed to get emotionally involved in the fates of their 'children'.

Iris could communicate with her 'daughter' Inneall at a distance. It was the mechanical genius of Inneall that had set up the communication and there was nothing unnatural about it. Iris now communicated to Inneall that she and her companions should create a disturbance or an 'Unusualness' to attract the attentions and presence of the Dolophonoi-Assassins. Then Iris and her fellow hunters would slip up to the nests of these killers and avail themselves of their weapons, and then set up an ambush nearby. The Dolophonoi always carried their usual weapons, their short-bladed sharp knives, with them; but Iris and her hunters would not have known how to battle with knives anyhow. Perhaps they could do some good with the unusual weapons of the Assassins, the big guns.

So it was done.

The Eleven Contemporaries, the Children of the Experiments, put on a circus; none of them was old enough (by quite a few decades) ever to have seen a circus, that's true. But Inneall had researched ancient circuses while on a nostalgia gig, and she had interested Henryetta in them also. Henryetta had then appealed to Inneall's surrogate grandfather Satrap Saint Ledger to buy them the steam calliope from the antique shop in Structo Lane. (Henryetta had no midas grandfather herself.)

Satrap bought the beautiful brass-tubed machine. And it was quickly rolled out and put to use. Henryetta could play it, and the only volume that the calliope had was loud. It was the sound of the steam calliope that brought the crowds of pleasure people from the whole shore to the circus, and it was the sound of the calliope that brought the assigned Dolophonoi-Assassins out of their nests in the rock cliffs to the popular Ocean Shore area. The Assassins did not recognize the sounds as music. But they were disturbing sounds, coming apparently from a gathering of their designated prey, and they had to investigate.

In the circus, all the animals were the Animals. Marino was the Seal. Lutin was the python-snake, the fortune-telling snake. Dubu was the bear. Schimp was the Chimp, Riesin the mother of the unborn Gajah was the Elephant, Carcajou was the Wolverene, Popugai was the Parrot. And all of them were natural-born performers, hams, comedians, incredible athletes and tricksters, consumate showpersons.

Ruddy Lord Randal in top hat and frock coat from an earlier era was ring-master. And Henryetta, riding on the head of Riesin the Mother Elephant, was the bespangled Queen of the Circus. They gave an amazing two hour performance there at Oceanside which had been Heart's Desire Cove before the lines of the Cove had been obliterated by the growing Ocean. And in the interval between circus performances, they split up into sideshows.

And the best of the sideshows was Lutin the Pythoness who predicted futures for all who came to her in her tent. She predicted by tarot cards, by crystal ball (which Satrap Saint ledger had bought for her in the antique shop in Structo Lane), by tea leaves, by palm reading, by skull-bump reading, by examining the entrails of birds which she whistled to come within her reach and then caught and tore asunder and spread out. She heckled the Dolophonoi to come to her and have their fortunes told, and the crowd joined her in heckling and bantering those Assassins. And one of them came in to her under the pressure of the heckling crowd.

"I see failure, failure, failure in the palms of your hands," Lutin gave her reading to that one. "Everything that you try on this mission will turn against you. I see you dead and dismantled if you do not abandon this mission at once. I see things more direful than this in your palms."

"Those are not my palms, girl snake," the Dolophonos said. "I am wearing gloves made from the hide of the gavial-crocodile of India. The gavial is not dead. It still roars with the pain of having these gloves cut out of his hide I wonder now how it would be if I had a pair of python-skin shoes cut from the hide of a living young pythoness? I could be the first in my set to have such shoes. It is part of the fearfulness that we project to mention such things that we have done and might do. Think of it, and you be fearful also!"

"I know not the word 'fear'," Lutin the Python-Snake said. "And I can see through every disguise that you wear whether on hands or feet or face. I see much more direful things coming to you than having painful pieces cut out of your skin. Think of it, and *you* be fearful."

"Give it up, little snake, give it up!" the Dolophonos spoke harshly and suddenly. "Disband your group and be yourself again, for a short while before you die. We ourselves are an indication that your Experiments will not work. We ourselves are the fruit of a false and forbidden Experiment using the same elements as are used in the Lynn-Randal and the other three Experiments. We are damnable mixtures of the human and the animal and the machine, and we have our roots in hell. Do you want to be like the Knives-Dolophonoi-Assassins; do you want to be like ourselves?"

"No, we do not," Lutin said firmly.

"Neither do we, but we are trapped in it," the Dolophonos spoke miserably. "You may fortune the fortunes as you will, but you cannot fortune your own. We will kill as many of your Three-Group, and of your Twelve-Group as we are able to. We cannot do otherwise. But, for your own good, break up your group before the end."

"We will not break it up. It is a good group," Lutin said.

The Dolophonos backed out of Lutin's tent in mixed fear and frustration and sorrow and anger. "I am going back to our nests to get the python-gun," he said. "This is intolerable."

An ordinary weapon would not kill a prophesying Python, but a Python-Gun would.

*   *   *   *

But the best act of the circus was not intended to be an act at all. It sprung up in the interval between the circus performances. It was an otherwordly sort of wrestling between Carcajou in his metamorphosized man-form and Luas the Angel. Some of the spectators at first believed (when the display had begun suddenly) that this wrestling was a sort of pyrotechnic display and that the 'wrestlers' were only moving figures drawn like hellish cartoons in the fire of a fire-works gala. There was the smell of black-powder and of gun-powder such as pyrotechnics does produce. And there was the smell of real brimstone over the whole area, strong, frightful. There was an animal howling, and a wolverene stench that complemented the brimstone. There was fire running over the limbs of both of the wrestlers. The eyes of the beholders were deceived and they did not know what they saw.

And there was indeed a dazzle on the two that confused the apperception. At first it seemed as if they were two boys wrestling. What else could it seem like? They were both just short of ten years old. Then it seemed as if they were two men wrestling, mighty and rampant men. And again it seemed as if they were two Titans wrestling, slightly fish-faced as are all Titans, somewhat bigger than giants, earth-shaking in their struggle.

"Then a man who was more than a man wrestled with him until it was after noon. He tried to escape from this wrestler so that he himself could become less than a man again, but he could not. And neither of them could prevail.

"The man who was more than a man touched the thigh of the other; and thereafter that other one could never change form again, nor go down on four legs like an animal again.

"'Have you done a good thing for me in revealing that this must be my true form?' asked he whose thigh had been touched.

"'Yes, I have done a good thing for you,' said the wrestler who was more than a man. 'I have cast it out of you, and now you are free from it. Perhaps I hear a call and must leave you now.'

"'You may not leave me till you bless me,' said he who could no longer go down like an animal.

"'No, it is you who must bless me,' said the man who was more than a man. He was an angel. And they wrestled no more. But strange persons who nested in the cliffs went to set their hands to weapons to try to kill both of them who had wrestled."

The Book of Jasher.

The others of the Eleven were amazed to find that the real form of Carcajou was that of a human and not that of a wolverene. So were the scanners of the neighborhood amazed. "Undocumented Human!" they gave their howl to their superior scanner, wherever it was. "Undocumented Human has appeared in inexplicable manner. Undocumented Mega Human!"

"I am going back to our nests to get an angel-gun," one of the Dolophonoi-Assassins said to another. "Neither short knife nor ordinary weapon will kill one of them. Only the angel-gun will kill that one, and it also kills the one who shoots it. But I was never told that this job would be free from danger."

"I am going back to our nest to get a wolverene-were gun." said the other Dolophonoi-Assassin. "With any other sort of gun, the person when shot can turn from one form to another and so escape. But the wolverene-were gun will kill him in both forms if they both bide in him. It will also kill werewolves and every sort of shape-changer. But again it kills the one who shoots it, so it will kill me in all my forms and disguises and manifestations. But neither was I ever told that this job would be free from danger."

Then those two Dolophonoi-Assassins also went back towards their nests in the cliffs to get the more deadly weapons.

Then the Mother Elephant Riesin, at the urging of her unborn daughter Gajah, began to crowd a fourth Dolophonoi who seemed to be newly assigned to the region and to the Children of the Experiments.

"You must leave this place," Riesin said. "You must leave this shore entirely. You are the one who owns the elephant gun. You will not confine yourself to monitoring the children. You mean to kill. I mean that you must leave this place entirely."

Riesin threatened to trample the Dolophonos, yes, but she always gave him a chance to escape as she drove him further and further away from what had once been Heart's Desire Cove.

"I will go back to our nests now and get the elephant-gun," this Dolophonoi-Assassin said. "This is intolerable. I will get the Elephant-Gun, and then I will kill you and yours, Dame Elephant."

*   *   *   *

The three monster-hunters, Iris Lynn-Randal, Shadrack Saleh, and Gregor McGregor, armed with the Python-gun, the Angel-gun, the Wolverene-were-gun, and the Elephant-gun, waited in ambush near the cliffs for the four Dolophonoi to return. They were resolved to kill those monsters. But they were fearful about the whole matter as the time came nearer. They had never killed, and it became more and more doubtful whether they could do it now.

The three of them began to tremble as they saw that they had been scented by the Assassins who now turned from the path leading to their cliff-nests, and came instead straight for the ambush.

"Shoot them now, shoot them now," Iris urged herself and her companions. But most of the persons who could kill had been eliminated from all ranks of the population below that of Mega Person, and none of these three was a Mega. Even before the leveling, the majority of the people were not able to kill.

89

Iris trembled. She sickened, and she tasted her own blood in her mouth. She moaned and prayed. And then she threw down the Python-Gun that she held. She wailed over her weakness.

Shadrack Saleh trembled and threw down the two guns that he held, the Angel-Gun and the Wolverene-were-Gun. He had doubly armed himself, and he was too weak to use the weapons.

Gregor McGregor trembled and tried to throw down the Elephant-Gun, but it stuck to his hands and he could not rid himself of it. He cried out with the pain of his hands that were cramped around the gun.

"No!" cried one of the Dolophonoi who broke roughly in the ambush now. "You cannot throw down the Elephant-Gun because you will be compelled to use it now. Your hands are like iron on it till you do use it. You have compelled us to advance the time, and the Mother Elephant has also compelled it. No, no, you will not shoot me with the Elephant-Gun. You point it in vain. And now you find that you are compelled to point it away from me. You will shoot the Mother Elephant Riesin, and you will shoot her unborn daughter Gajah in her belly. And you will kill them both. Riesin stands clearly in the open now. You have a good shot from here. The Elephant-Gun is directed by the will, and it cannot miss if the one who shoots it wills that it shall hit.

"No!" Gregor cried. "I do not will that I shoot, and I do not will that I hit."

"Something is churning in your will though," the Dolophonos said. "It would be wonderful for me to kill the Elephants and you could not stop me from it. But it is more wonderful that I compel you to do it, that I compel you to *will* to do it. Aim and fire!"

"No!" Gregor cried out. "Gajah is my adopted daughter and Riesin is her mother. Riesin is an Empress Elephant, and Gaja is a 'Wonder of the World' Elephant."

"We know that," the Dolophonos spoke impatiently. 'We are not in the business of killing *ordinary* Elephants. Aim and shoot!"

"I will shoot myself first."

"You may not do that," the Assassin said. "You're doomed to hang rather. You are under a compulsion. You can shoot the two-in-one Elephants but no other thing. You've no choice. Aim and fire!"

Under the strange compulsion, Gregor McGregor willed to

kill the Elephants. He aimed and fired with a horrible, roaring, echoing, beastly noise. Riesin the Mother Elephant staggered, but she did not go down. Nevertheless, Gregor knew for certain that he had killed the unborn daughter Gajah, a 'Wonder of the World' Elephant.

He threw down the Elephant-Gun then. The compulsion was finished. He broke out of the ambush and ran back into the wastelands on the north shore of Inneall's Ocean. Then, in his running and raving mad state, Gregor came to a carob tree and hung himself on it till he was dead. The carob is that pretty Mediterranean evergreen that is sometimes called the 'Judas Tree', one of the ornamental trees that had been used to beautify the old strip pits there.

The other two hunters were wandering in the waste-lands also, broken in mind and spirit.

And back at the circus, the steam calliope was still playing, horribly loud, horribly beautiful.

CHAPTER NINE

ON THE SHIP *ANNABELLA SAINT LEDGER*

Oh vengeful balls-of-fire and hail!
The Kangaroo in motion!
The Land is red in tooth-and-nail;
We'll hide upon the Ocean.
Annabella Saint Ledger Pirate Chantey

Riesin was an Empress Elephant. In earlier days in India, Empress Elephants used to serve as mayors of villages and towns and even of very large cities. They were very good mayors, being honest, intelligent, diligent, compassionate, fair, foresightful, and of outgoing and magnetic personalities. Moreover they were stable and not given to flightiness.

When travelers would come to a town, if they saw that it was well-kept and beautiful and busy and of happy-and-singing inhabitants, they would say "This town has an Empress Elephant for Mayor." But if they saw that the town was unkempt and weed-choked and with the roads and streets broken, and that the inhabitants were ill-disposed, they would say "This town has a Human Mayor. There are just not enough Empress Elephants for every town to have one; and an ordinary Elephant does not make any better mayor than a human would."

But when the Moguls came to India as conquerors and despoilers, the Empress Elephants tried to get their towns to stand fast against the fierce invaders. They failed, and the Moguls slew all the Empress Elephants. And the custom of having Empress Elephants for mayors was never renewed.

But Empress Elephants, even if hurt unto death, will always know what they must do. The Empress Elephant Riesin walked north, painfully and as if she were drunken, through the hill-lands and tangled waste-lands north of Inneall's Ocean, and she knew exactly where she was going.

Satrap Saint Ledger had set up a double scanner in the big clubroom that he shared with Livius Secundus and Felix Culebra y Columba in Structo Lane. The Ten Children of the Experiment (both Axel and Gajah were lost from the original Twelve now, and Luas himself was saying that he himself must go very soon)—the Ten Children had come to Satrap there for they were bewildered and without a leader. They watched on the double scanner.

One side of the scanner showed Riesin trudging in great apparent pain northward through that wasteland above Inneall's Ocean. The other side of the scanner showed a rocky road traversing high foothills that stood before very high mountains.

"As you see," Satrap told the Ten, "Riesin the mother of the unborn Gajah has started northward to the Graveyard of the Elephants in India, to bury (they bury under piles of brush and not in the ground) the dead one she is carrying, and to die herself."

"But this isn't India," Inneall-Annabella protested.

"There is a jog in the road," answered Satrap who had a touch of the mystic in him, "and by that jog an Elephant may pass from a road in midland America to a road in India. The Graveyard of the Elephants is in the small realm of Mustang just north of India in the high foothills of the higher mountains. You can see a bit of the road leading to it, and you can see a part of the Elephant Graveyard on the second side of the scanner-scope. I have a man there. I'll get him on the voxo, and he'll go to the spot we are watching. He'll tell us when Riesin is coming to it, when she accomplishes the jog in the road. Then we can witness her last sad acts."

"The real name of these last days and years is 'The Fulfillment of the World'," Livius Secundus the Ambulatory Computer whose passion was history told them. "The 'Fulfillment of the World' isn't easy. There are persons and beings and contrivances who would block the fulfillment of the world. One of them is coming now. But all these things of the latter days, the Computer Machines that are made in the image of Man as Man is made in the image of God, the readying of 'Second Humanity' for possible awakening, the rising of geniused animals with their trans-animal talents for speech and abstract thought and role-

playing, all these things are part of the 'Fulfillment and Enlargement of the World'. But, as I say, the enemies of the fulfillment
and enlargement are upon us everywhere, and one of them is
even now at the door."

One of them came through the door. He had the aura and
odor of a Dolophonos-Assassin, but he had a more powerful
presence than any of the others had had. He came and stood
just behind the young man Carcajou, he who that morning had
still seemed to be a young wolverene. Well, the wolverene-devil
has been cast out of him now. It was Carcajou of whom the
scanners of the neighborhood had howled "Undocumented
Human! Undocumented Mega Human!" a few hours before.
Well, this was a Mega Dolophonos who had been sent to dispose
of Carcajou somehow. The Mega Dolophonos sneered and
smiled, touched Carcajou on the shoulder so that livid white
sparks of fire jumped between them, and Carcajou groaned and
slumped foreward in pain. The Mega Dolophonos laughed a
chilling laugh and went out again for a while.

An Asiatic of the strong-nosed Aryan type appeared on the
second side of the scanner-scope. He waved to Satrap Saint
Ledger and to all of them. "She is coming up the rocky road
now," said the man in Hindi; and all of them, having intelligences clear off the scale and accomplishments to match, understood him. "She is dying on her feet, but she will accomplish
her mission. You can hear her labored breathing and groaning
now."

And they could hear it. And in a very short while they saw
the Empress Elephant Riesin herself on the scope. She was blood-
covered, and she breathed out bloody foam. She found a clean
spot and quickly brought forth the dead Gajah. Then she pulled
small bushes with her trunk, and all the watchers knew without
being told (except for their odor that came from the scanner-
scope) that they were Himalaya Incense Bushes. Riesin covered
Gajah up with the incense bushes and fronds. Then three flames
came down from the middle air and hovered over Gajah. "They
will burn over her for thirty days," Satrap Saint Ledger said.
"I will burn over her much longer than that. She was indeed
a 'Wonder of the World' Elephant."

Riesin staggered a score of steps up the path beyond Gajah.
Then she lay down and died with a great sigh. The Asiatic of
the strong-nosed Aryan type, he who was in the employ of Satrap
Saint Ledger, took up a double-bladed axe and began to cut

94

boughs from the Mountain Yew Trees and to cover Riesin with them.

The trick of bi-location or trans-location, used by the India Elephants to cover hundreds and thousands of miles when they are dying and are impelled to find the Elephant Graveyard, is not unknown in other contexts. Hubbard, in his *'Big Book of Strange Happenings'* lists eleven cases of this happening to humans. There was the case of a man walking up a street in the Intramuros District of Manila deep in daydreaming. Then, when he came to himself, he was walking up a street in the Embarcadero District of San Francisco. He knew the neighborhoods in both cities well. He had close friends in both places. And it was verified by them that he had been in Manila at such a time and in San Francisco at such a time fifteen minutes later. And the other cases cited in the *'Big Book of Strange Happenings'* were very like this first case. The common elements were that the person had to know both places, either for their fame or for his own acquaintance of them, and that he had to be completely raptured in a daydream when it happened. Then a jog in the undermind will correspond with a jog in the road, and the trans-location will be effected.

Migrating birds sometimes do this also. A bird may be winging south on his migration (especially such a bird as a Swift or a Swallow) over the plains of Nebraska, deep in a daydream (birds are notoriously deep day-dreamers), and then the bird will be winging south over the thick forests of Honduras. But it isn't a really common happening with any species, or it wasn't up till the Second Day of Summerset of that particular year.

*   *   *   *

"Satrap, my surrogate grandfather," Inneall-Annabella said. "We want you to buy that brass cannon and all seven of its cannon-balls that are in the antique shop up the Lane."

"And please mount it on the ship *Annabella Saint Ledger* immediately," Henryetta ordered in her preemptory way. "We are going to make that ship our headquarters, so we want the best weapon that your money can buy for our protection."

"That old brass cannon is not the best weapon that my money can buy," Satrap said. "For defense it is useless."

"My researches tell me otherwise," Inneall contradicted.

"It's an enchanted cannon, you see," Henryetta explained. "The cannon-balls are really annihilation shells. And, while the

95

charges of the cannon would ordinarily be too weak to lob the cannon-balls more than two or three miles, yet they will really go as far as they are ordered to go, even around the curve of the Earth. And they will hit whatever they are ordered to hit. In addition to that, the cannon-balls are self-perpetuating. No matter how many of them are shot off, there will still be the original seven of them left. This is the special ninety-ninth cannon that was on the Golden Hind, the most feared pirate ship of them all. The other ninety-eight cannons were for appearance only, but this enchanted ninety-ninth cannon did all the damage. If we have it mounted, we can whip anything on the Ocean."

"You two come at me so sharply with your demands that I might as well have both of you for surrogate granddaughters," Satrap mused. "I'll adopt you too, Henryetta, in the same irregular fashion that I adopted Inneall."

"No, I'll not be adopted even irregularly. I was born an orphan and I'll die an orphan."

"Where were you raised, Henryetta?"

"For the first sixteen months of my life I was at the Main Waif-arama in Los Angeles. It's the biggest Waif-arama in the world. In the sixteen months I was there, the Main Waif-arama had eight different buildings and locations, but always at the same general location. Sour-Grass Park West. The Waif-arama burned down seven times, and when I say 'down' I do mean 'down', all the way down. Each building was built better and more fireproof than those before it, and the next-to-last one was built entirely out of asbestos fire-brick and had not an ounce of anything in it that could possibly be set on fire. Nevertheless it burned to the ground. Well really, it burned so hotly that it burned a hole pretty deep in the ground."

"Were you the fire-bug, Henryetta?"

"Yes. I was just nine days old when I discovered that I had the talent for setting things on fire from a distance. I did it because I had frustrations. Were *you* ever a little baby? It's maddening. But I could set fires with my towering mentality at any distance and to any extent, no matter how total."

"And when you had burned down seven Main Waif-aramas and were housed in the eighth, then what happened, Henryetta?"

"I was only in the eighth one for one day after we moved into it from the tents. Then they told me that I'd get the best assignment that anyone ever had, and that I'd be with my equals in intelligence, something that had never been the case before. 'All right,' I said. So I joined the Wintergreen-Luna Experiment with the young Seal named Marino and the young Angel named Luas. I've never had any regrets about joining them. I see a bit of dubiety in your eye, pseudo-grandfather Satrap. What would you like to see burned?"

"This wotto-metal statue of the 'Unknown Animal'. Wotto-metal as a matter of definition, is unburnable."

The wotto-metal statuette burst into sudden hot flame and it was reduced to writhing ashes within three seconds. And the ashes were reduced into nothingness in another three seconds.

"That's the trouble with Unknown Animals," Henryetta said. "Now it'll always be unknown."

"I'm impressed, Henryetta," Satrap Saint Ledger admitted. "Inneall-Annabella, I've always thought that you were the 'child' who could do anything. Could you have burned that wotto-metal statue as well? Could you have burned down seven Waif-arama buildings as well?"

"Oh yes. I could have burned them all as well by using only my subtle mentality. But I couldn't have narrated them as well."

"I surrender completely," Satrap conceded. "What else do you two demand for the ship?"

"That the steam calliope be moved onto the ship," Henryetta ordered. "We can use it to scare all the other ships and all evil spirits away. The always-reappearing Flying Dutchman has such a calliope on board, and persons who see that Ghost Ship think that it is damned souls howling."

"That's what I thought it was the last time I saw Old Dutch," Satrap admitted. "All right, I'll have the calliope put on board. What else do you two demand for the Ship?"

"Those seven one-hundred-gallon drums of Invisible Paint that are in the antique shop up the Lane," Inneall-Annabella stated. "Have them put on the ship before dark, and we'll paint the ship with it in the dark. The paint doesn't go well unless it's applied in the dark."

"Inneall-Annabella, that paint is a fake," Satrap Saint Ledger said. "There is nothing at all in those seven one-hundred gallon drums that are marked Invisible Paint. The drums are empty. Even the proprietor of the shop admits that. It's true that there is an anomaly of gravity connected with the seven drums. They are as heavy as if they were full of paint, but I assure you that they are completely empty."

"No, fake grandfather, no," Henryetta protested. "They are full of Invisible Paint, and we will paint the *Annabella Saint Ledger* with that Invisible Paint. Please buy the seven big drums of paint and have them put on board. And buy eleven good brushes also."

"Why eleven? There are only ten of you now, since Axel and Gajah are no longer in your company."

"Our researches tell us that Invisible Alfred lives in one of the drums," Inneall-Annabella explained. "Well, if he is a stow-away, then he shall earn his way. Let him paint too. He is no better than the rest of us. The eleventh brush will be for Invisible Alfred."

* * * *

Three of the Pirate Crewmen from the Ship *Annabella Saint Ledger* came down to Structo Alley to the fine condominium of Satrap Saint Ledger and Livius Secundus and Felix Culebra y Columba. They would discuss what was really required to fit the ship for any eventuality.

The three pirate crewmen were named Lanternjaw Lunnigan, Sebastian Lazar, and Quentillius Quern the Fifth.

"I have wondered about your names as I've seen them on the ship's manifest," Satrap Saint Ledger said. "They seem con-trived."

"My name is my own," Lanternjaw Lunnigan said, "and my given name is my mother's surname. I am descended from Hosea Lanternjaw of Surrey in England. The Lanternjaws have been a pirate family for many centuries, and my great-great-grand-father Gammon Lanternjaw pirated well into the twentieth cen-tury. Of the other two pirate seamen here though, their names are indeed contrived. The name of Sebastian Lazar was given to this salt-water person here by the little contraption Inneall. And the name Quentillius Quern the Fifth was given to this other person by the little girl Henryetta. These two Royal Kids thought that the names they gave sounded like pirate names. The original names of the two seamen, Hector Brown and Jasper Jones apparently did not."

"Several of the Dolophonoi-Assassins are practicing directed somnambulistic activities," the pirate seaman Sebastian Lazar said. "They'll be able to carry out somnambulistic killing then, sleep-walking killing. They're effective enough killers when they're wide awake. Does their proposed sleep-walking killing mean anything to any of you?"

"Not a thing, not a thing, but I'll put my back brain to work on the information," Satrap said. "I've wondered about the vesture of you seamen also. It likewise seems pretty contrived."

"It's the same two Royal Kids with the same two fingers sticking into the pot, sir," Lanternjaw explained. "It's Inneall and Henryetta again. They had the duds sent to the ship by a costumer. They thought that they looked like pirate duds. Our honest ship garberdines apparently did not. The costumes are all right except that they are too high-and-binding in the crotch. 'I want my pirates to be high-stepping pirates,' is what that grinning Inneall there said. Well, you'll step pretty high when you wear those high-crotched duds, or you'll suffer for not doing it. You're all right if you don't put your feet all the way down to the deck, I suppose."

"I kind of like the looks of them," Satrap commented, "contrived or not. And I also like my pirates to be high-stepping pirates. Now, have you any specific recommendations as to the food-and-drink on the ship?"

"It's all right except on Mondays, Wednesdays, and Fridays," Lanternjaw spoke carefully. "On those three days, instead of rations we have only Inneall's directive: 'Lettum live this day on the fish they catch themselves.' Ah, midas Satrap, pirates aren't very good fishermen. We can pull in lots of stuff, but little of it is tasty. This is 'New Ocean' so far, and pretty roiled, and many of the best fish haven't followed it here yet. And then there's the rum. 'Pirates are supposed to drink rum,' this urchin Inneall says and also writes in her memos. 'They're supposed to drink hogsheads and hogsheads of it. The rum of the Indies, that's what.' Midas man, there are other drinks besides rum, and we should have our choice. And it is only the worst of the rum that is coopered into hogsheads or butts or pipes or tuns. The best rum always comes in bottles, haven't you noticed that? After all, this isn't the fifteenth century. And then there's the question of live provender, especially the giant, live ocean-turtles, more than three hundred of them in the aft hold right now. There are more things in the world than turtle soup or even than turtle steak. And then there's the honey bees alive and loose in the midship hold. 'Find where they have their hives,' Inneall says in her memos, 'and take the honey out of them, and make mead or honey wine out of it.' Listen, those bees were thrown into that hold by some jokers. They don't have any honey. They don't have any hive or home. They'd like to go home but they don't know how to get out of the hold. But they sure will sting you if you go into that midship hold at all. And then there's the live cape buffalos in the fore hold. Dammit there's no tougher meat this side of hell than cape buffalo meat."

"I have here three sharp, short-bladed knives for three Royal Kids, Ruddy Lord Randal and Carcajou and Schimp," Quentillius Quern the Fifth said. "These three knives were taken off dead Dolophonoi-Assassins and they are well broken-in. They will kill Dolophonoi. Most knives won't bite into them at all." The Quentillius gave a knife to each of them, to Lord Randal and Carcajou and Schimp. That was the kind of gift that was appreciated, knives that were already blooded and broke in.

"There is also the way the dispensery and infirmary are run on the *Annabella Saint Ledger*," Sebastian Lazar broke in. "It's all governed by a single directive which reads: 'For any sickness or suppuration, lettum drink bilge-water tonic.' I think that's another gem of Inneall's."

"No, it's a gem of mine," Henryetta said. "It's the universal cure-all for sick pirates, bilge-water tonic, and bilge-water tonic again."

"All these things are trifles," Satrap Saint Ledger said. "In general, how are things, and how is the attitude of the crew?"

"Oh, everything's perfect," Lanternjaw Lunnigan chirped. "Perfect," piped Sebastian Lazar. "Perfect," echoed Quentillius Quern the Fifth. "There was never such a satisfied crew since the world began. We'll follow these Royal Kids (that's what we call them) forever. We'll follow the whole bunch of them all the way to hell if it comes to that. There was never a happier bunch than weselves."

* * * *

"Midas-man Satrap Saint Ledger, did you ever hear of Tom Dooley's Island?" Sebastrian Lazar asked.

"Yes, I owned it when it was Tom Dooley's Hill, and I still own it when Inneall's Ocean has circumvallated it and made it an island. I have a good solid home on it, spacious and pleasant."

"But is it pleasant? The Island is sinking, you know. It's been sinking for an hour. And before the coming night is over with, it will be thirty fathoms deep under the new ocean."

"Whence have you these times and measurements, pirate?"

"From the little pythoness there in the corner. That's what she has predicted, and we have come to trust her predictions. I think we had better calk and waterproof the house so that the Royal Kids can use it after the Island is submerged. All the really important Pirate Moguls have had their secret houses *under the Ocean*. Oh really, there's no way they could be first-class without it."

"What will it take?" Satrap asked.

"Thirty tons of calking compound. And an alley oop thirty-three fathoms long. We may as well make provisions for high tides."

"All right. Get the stuff and do the job. Charge it to 'Ship's Stores'. Quentillius the Fifth, I understand that you are in charge of loading consignments onto the ship and making them fast. We have certain things to load by nightfall."

"Aye, the brass cannon and the cannon-balls, the steam calliope, the seven one-hundred-gallon drums of Invisible Paint. The thirty tons of calking compound and the one thousand pounds of hamburger meat. That's to give us a change from live-turtle meat. And five thousand rounds of bazooka shells just to be sure that we have plenty. Everything will be loaded on and made fast, applied, refrigerated, fried, put on steam, or otherwise processed according to its nature and circumstance. And we might take on two hundred kilograms of blood plasma. Pirates bleed a lot when they're in bloody combat."

"All right. See to it. But seriously, fellows, could we repel a professional attack?" Satrap asked.

"Oh absolutely!" Lanternjaw assured him. "We could repel almost any sort of attack; and we could counter-attack any invaders all the way to the bottom of the ocean. We have rifles and automatic rifles, 90-mm point-blank pieces, bazookas, and directional cluster-bombs. Besides that we'll have the enchanted cannon. Aye, and we'll have the 'Ship Invisible' after the Royal Kids get it painted with the invisible paint. That's really a big advantage. Those things actually do work, midas-man Satrap Saint Ledger."

"There are eleven wolverenes making a disturbance outside," a courier announced, sticking his head inside the clubroom. "Do they belong to anybody in here, or shall we kill them?"

*   *   *   *

"First the whales, and now the wolverenes," Lanternjaw Lunnigan said. "The whales have already moved into this part of the ocean, though it's really too shallow for them. For them to have real fun at their diving and sounding, they need water at least a mile deep. Well, maybe they're shallow-bottom whales. Whatever the whales are, they're building something. They're constructing something under water, and just about half a mile from the south end of Tom Dooley's Island."

"The wolverenes have come for me," Carcajou said, and he was shaking with fright. "They want to take me back with them. They want to take me back into their form, and I don't want to go."

"You have your knife, Carcajou," Marino the Seal said. "Ruddy Lord Randal has his, and Schimp has his. These knives will kill wolverenes, who are devils, just as they will kill Dolophonoi. I have my teeth, and Popugai has his sheep-killing beak. We five have never yet enjoyed the fellowship of going together into a really rousing battle. Let's enjoy it now and rip up the eleven wolverenes."

But the roaring and howling and devil-yelling of the eleven wolverenes shook all of Structo Lane and scared everybody, even those who laughed and affected not to take it heavily.

"Oh, but one of the wolverenes is myself in my other form," Carcajou cried out, "and we won't know which one. He'll hide in the middle of the other ten, and if we kill him, we'll kill me also."

"No, he is not you," Luas the young angel said. "He is only a devil-animal who inhabited you for some years and forced you to take his form. But he has been cast out of you. If you let him come back into you though, your last state will be worse than your first. I will go out and deal with them."

"You cannot wrestle with all eleven of them at one time, Luas." Carcajou warned.

"Yes, in my own way I can wrestle with eleven of them at once," Luas said softly, and he went out. Then the noise and menace of the wolverenes became threefold as strong as it had been before.

"I'm glad we don't have those wolverenes on the Ocean," Lanternjaw Lunnigan said. "They spook me. I'm even a little bit afraid of bears, if you'll pardon me for the feeling, Dubu. A pirate ship I was once on tangled with another pirate ship named 'The Unrepentent Rascal'; the Unrepentent had a big Alaskan

Brown Bear for first mate, and he sure sent shivers down the backs of all of us. He was a slow man with the cutlass though and also with the ship's sword, pardon me again Dubu. Ah, we had bear steak for a week after that encounter."

"Somewhere there are three ugly sisters sitting in an ugly room with straw on the floor of it," Lutin the girl pythoness was saying. "To people who have their eyes put in backwards, the three sisters are beautiful. But I see them true and I see them ugly. One of them, Clotho, spins out threads from the straw on the floor for each of us here. The second one, Lachesis, measures the threads, and I believe that she is dooming the threads of several of us to be long enough. The third sister, Atropos, cuts the threads with her scissors when her sister has measured them to their full length. And I feel that Atropos has her avid scissors in her hand now. There is antipathy between those three sisters and all pythons everywhere from the beginning of the world."

"We are only concerned with menaces on board the *Annabella Saint Ledger*," Sebastian Lazar said.

"But, among other places, they *are* on board the *Annabella*," Lutin sighed one of her weary snake-sighs.

"Oh, *that* ugly room, and *those* three ugly sisters!" Lanternjaw turned his attention to the matter. "we'll thwart them somehow."

The roaring and howling of the wolverenes broke into separate pieces and rushed away. The eleven noises could be heard diminishing as they went into the distance. Then they were muted and muffled as if their roaring had gone underwater. And Luas the Angel came back in.

"What did you do, Luas?" Schimp asked. "How did you defeat them?"

"I turned them into devil-fish," Luas said, "and they had to rush into the ocean before they drowned in the air. But they'll still roar at you when you're in the good ship *Annabella Saint Ledger*. And now I must go."

"You reduce our number if you go," Inneall said sadly.

"No. I was never really of your number. I was an observer only. Most of us will meet again in the better place. I hope it is all of us, but several of you are tricky." And Luas was gone.

All of them went out to Oceanside then, where the good ship *Annabella Saint Ledger* was being loaded with her mixed cargo of ship's stores and supplies. And then themselves loaded on. They sailed into the evening-blue Ocean with a flapping of sails and a braying of donkey engines. And almost immediately the Intrepid Nine (their number was reduced by three by this time) broke out the barrels of Invisible Paint and dangled their trestles over the side and began to paint the hull of the ship. This was necessary if the ship was to be able to hide from its enemies even in clear water and bright sunshine. But the concealing paint would only have its full effect if applied in the dark.

Invisible Alfred was roused out of his barrel. He was not completely invisible unless he closed both his mouth and his eyes at the same time. His eyes were visible when he had them open, and the inside of his mouth was visible when he talked.

The Nine Intrepid Royal Kids painted all the night and were finished just as the false dawn came an hour before the true dawn of morning. It had been the Second Night of Summerset that was just ending.

* * * *

There are those who have found certain extravagances of detail in these true narrations taken from the true logs of Four Experiments and One Noble Ship and Two Lanes and one House that sank to the bottom of the Ocean. No, everything is accurate. It is that there is a lack of extravagance seen by those who wear blinders on their eyes. But things seen true do have this authentic extravagance and exuberance always.

CHAPTER TEN

THE WHALES ARE BUILDING SOMETHING

Before the Whales had lost their legs
They built in deepest ocean dregs.

The Whales build grand, they build galore:
Build Castles on the Ocean Floor.

The Whales build forts of Ocean Stone;
Build stronger forts than Carcassonne.

The Whales build fair with glad and glee;
Build Mansions underneath the Sea.

The Whales build straight by rule-of-thumb;
Build Palaces in Kingdom Come.
                    The Child's Big Book of Whales.
                                          Anon.

  "I love to sail the ocean quaint
   I love the waves that rush-o.
   I love to paint with sightless paint,
   I love to whack my brush-o."
              Ballad of Invisible Alfred

"The great underwater City of Lyonesse off of Land's End
in Brittany of France has amazed all the ocean-archeologists.
It has been called the City of Giants and the City of Titans.
Why are these great halls and corridors and arcades and
concourses so large? Why are the stone couches (for they
are nothing else) twenty times the length of a man? Why
are the stone risers of the huge staircases thirty feet in
height?

"There are some who say that Lyonesse was indeed built by the Titans when, after they were overthrown by the Gods of Olympus, they fled from their ancestral inner sea to the outer ocean. There are some who say that the City was built by the Sons of Anak, the Giants of the Old Testament.

"But I believe that it was built by whales."

The Back Door of History.   Arpad Arutinov.

When false dawn had turned into true and the sky was whitening (this was on the early morning of the Second Day of Summerset), it could be seen that the whales, who had arrived in that extreme part of Inneall's Ocean only the day before, were making a great turmoil in the water.

They were diving, they were sounding, they were bringing up mud and dregs from the bottom of the still-shallow Ocean.

"They will kill themselves ramming their heads and mouths into the too-shallow bottom," Livius Secundus the Ambulatory Computer who was also an historian said. "Cannot someone talk to the whales and explain to them that it's too shallow? Can you talk to whales, Marino?"

"Sure," said Marino the Seal. "Can't you?"

"I had the Ocean here sounded yesterday," Satrap Saint Ledger answered. "It was three furlongs deep (three-eighths of a mile deep) at its shallowest place. And it's deeper now. It's growing deeper every day. If it were deeper, the whales would hit bottom even harder. They can't get up proper speed in even a half mile. They're excavating, you see."

"Excavating for what, Satrap?" Livius Secundus asked.

"I don't know. To get down to bed-rock I suppose. And the 'big lime' is bed-rock here and isn't very deep. They will build a Castle or Palace or Monument of some sort. All we can guess is that it will be huge and that its architecture will be Contemporary Oceanic. I'm trafficking in limestone with them. They've already taken most of the really big limestones, and now they're dealing with four other building-rock firms as well as my own."

"How did you set up a deal like that, Satrap?"

"Dolphins were the middlemen. They brought in a squid-skin tarp that was floated by several hundred blow-fish bladders. It had about three hundred pounds of nugget ocean gold on it. They wanted all the big limestones they could get for that much gold. We've been loading them on tip-barges for several hours and taking them out and dumping them at the designated places in the ocean. I've delivered about a thousand tons of big limestone since midnight, and the other four building-stone firms have probably delivered another thousand tons. They'll have the start of some pretty big structures done before this morning is over with. I enjoy doing business with the whales. They're real gentlemen."

"Has this anything to do with Tom Dooley Island, Satrap?"

"I don't know, Livius. The whales seem to be building their thing about a half mile from Tom Dooley's Island itself."

"According to the Pythoness the island will sink into the ocean today, but so far it is riding in the water as high as it was yesterday. But there seems to be something gone wrong with Tom Dooley's Island. Parts of it go out. They just aren't there for a while. And then they are there again."

"Oh, that's only the good ship *Annabella Saint Ledger*, Livius. The Royal Kids painted it with invisible paint during the night. When it comes between us and Tom Dooley's Island, it makes that part of the island invisible, blocks it out with its own bulk. The ship isn't really invisible, of course. It's only about ninety-nine percent invisible. But the paint does conceal it pretty well from enemies. And I'm afraid that it will have many enemies this day and tomorrow."

"What kind of enemies, Satrap?"

"Oh, the Principalities and Powers, that sort of thing."

*   *   *   *

"This clown, this Joker, can he plan, can he think, can he handle situations, has he a good name with good people? This clown, does he have brains?"

Enniscorthy Chronicle.

Invisible Alfred announced himself to be a Prophet—"aye, and more than a Prophet. For I am he for whom the endless ages have yearned, and whoever comes to me will not go away empty."

On the Ship *Annabella Saint Ledger*, the howling of the devil-fish who had been wolverenes was an offense to the ears and dispositions of everybody on board. Not only did they roar like wolverenes and devils and sea-satans, but they also taunted in human voices. "Throw Carcajou to us," they bantered. "Throw Ruddy Lord Randal to us. Throw Inneall to us. We'll tear them to pieces in their bodies and brains and souls and essences. We'll eat them

107

alive, we'll eat them dead. Throw them to us!" Well, the cries were piercing, and all the people on the *Annabella Saint Ledger* had blood running out of their ears on account of them. And that is why, when Invisible Alfred began to preach, Ruddy Lord Randal called out to Alfred: "If you must preach, Invisible Alfred, preach to those damned Devil-Fish. Are not your own invisible ears bleeding invisible blood on account of them also. Teach them a little deportment. Preach and pray that they receive the gift of silence."

"Their voices bother you?" Invisible Alfred asked as if amazed. "But all voices on Earth and in the Ocean praise me whenever they sound, whether they intend it or not. All of them rebound to my glory. Rather than pray that they may receive the gift of silence, I will pray that you receive the gift of patience." Invisible Alfred spoke with power and softness. (Notice sometimes that all Prophets have such ambiguous voices.) "But that you may know that I have the power—I will quiet the Devil-Fishes for a little while only. I was not sent to save Devils but honest People and Machines and Animals. But that you may know that I have the Power over Devils also—

"Be quiet, Devil-Fish. I place an impediment on the tongue of each one of you. Hold your peace and make no more outcry for a while. I will tell you when you may give voice again."

And unaccountably the eleven Devil-Fish, they who had been the eleven Devil-Wolverenes, fell silent. The silence was so sudden and so total that it might almost have been called an echoing silence.

There was no doubt that Invisible Alfred scored in this. But to be a success in the Prophesying-and-Denouncing business, one must score again and again. Besides that, Alfred was wasted on the small number of witnesses, only the Royal Kids and the Pirate Crew of the Ship. But he took steps to increase his crowd and to speak from his weird advantage. Though neither his eyes nor the inside of his mouth were very good, yet the fact that they were the only things of him ever seen was an advantage. Yes, but he'd have come on stronger if he'd had stronger eyes. But no Prophet has everything, and he did use his ambiguous Prophet's Voice well.

"Captain and Crewmen!" he cried out now in his dubious voice, "put the ship in to the Ocean Shore where the depth of the water comes right up to the shore bank." It is nearly certain that Invisible Alfred had just heard Lord Randal give that exact order, to put in to shore at that exact place. But Alfred took advantage of it, and he spoke as the ship went there:

"There are three great places from which crowds may be addressed: from strategic balconies overlooking vast plazas, from mountains with green slopes where crowds may recline, and from ships brought right up to land. But the strategic balcony is not available to me, nor was it to the Christus. The balconies are for the rich and the powerful, not for poor and barefoot Prophets. Believe me that I *am* barefooted though my feet are invisible to you. And the ideal mountain is not at hand. I could ask for it, of course, and it would be given to me, but that would be too great a sign to give you this day. So I will speak from shipboard, as did the Christus often. Captain and Crewmen, slew the Ship around on its holding kedge anchor and bring it aft to the shore. I will talk to the multitudes from this high little poop deck."

Invisible Alfred had just heard Lord Randal give the order to slew the ship about on its kedge anchor and bring it aft to the shore, but the people on shore couldn't have heard Lord Randal's order. And they did hear the words of Invisible Alfred.

"Repent, ye multitudes, and listen to my words," Invisible Alfred now spoke directly to the crowd that was gathering on shore, attracted by the novelty of him. "Let your ears be circumcised so you can hear me better! Know you how I became what I am, how I became the Invisible Alfred? Like Jonah, a fellow Prophet, I spent three days in the belly of a whale. It was from that experience that my skin became whited (from the digestive juices in the whale's stomach) and of no color at all, it was from that experience that I became so colorless that I was already half invisible."

Some of the people in the gathering crowd laughed in a way that Invisible Alfred might not exactly have wished for. The Pleasure People who were spending the day at New Oceanside, at the part of it which had been named Heart's Desire Cove when it was still a Cove, had already thronged to the shore in the number of ten thousand. There was a natural amphitheatre there in the folding of the hills and it always seemed easy to gather a crowd into it. These people liked to be entertained, and they liked to cross words with the mountebanks.

"Hey, All-Eyes-And-Mouth," someone in the crowd called out, "you don't look like much. What did the *whale* look like after he'd voided you?"

109

"I'll show you," Invisible Alfred spoke with his soft power, and he stretched out his hand. A really magnificent whale broke the glassy smooth surface of the Ocean, bowed himself clear of the water, and spouted a rousing royal spout of water and steam as he fell back. Invisible Alfred had scored again. And he went with confidence into his rigamarole.

"Repent, you the multitudes, and listen to my words," he spoke with his strong and flexible voice that he could pop like a whip. "After I had been three nights and three days in the whale's belly, I spent nine thousand years in a one-hundred-gallon drum that had held invisible paint before it was emptied. From the residue of the invisible paint, I drew the power of near-invisibility. Full invisibility is never given all at once. Know you though that near-invisibility is a two-sided gift. The more nearly invisible a person becomes, the more nearly are all things visible to that person. Even your most invisible thoughts are not invisible to me. I see them all.

"I know which ones of you are good and which ones of you are evil; and I know which ones of you need be evil no longer. It is to you people of the third condition that I say 'Repent! Repent!' and again 'Repent!'

"You think that I am funny-looking because only my eyes are visible to you. Only my eyes, and the inside of my mouth when I open it to utter words of wisdom. Know you that this was also the appearance of God himself when he spoke to Moses out of the Burning Bush, when he spoke out of the Whirlwind, when he spoke on the Mountain of the Commandments. Only his eyes could be seen, and the inside of his mouth when he uttered words. And the words themselves could be seen when they came out of his mouth, bright and winged words. So are my words bright and winged if only you have the ears to hear and the eyes to see."

Some of the people began to laugh. Oh, Invisible Alfred had scored points, but there was something lacking. It was a stroke of genius that only his eyes should be visible. But it didn't work as well as it might have, because he had weak and washed-out eyes.

"Shall I give you another sign?" he popped his voice like a whip. He had some good tricks he could do with his voice, but a limited number of them. "Shall I map the heavens to you in broad daylight?" he asked. "Will you understand it even if I do? Behold then the zone and girdle of the heavens! Please dim

110

the sun a little bit. Good!"

The sun did dim, though there were not any clouds in the sky, nor did Invisible Alfred call any clouds into being. But he did cause the zone and girdle of the heavens to appear, the circle of signs, the circle of animals, the zodiac. The Twelve Constellations were too high above the horizons for verisimilitude. And in strict accuracy, some of them should have been *below* the horizon. But they did appear clearly, even shockingly and garishly, in the sky of the curious dimmed sun: Aries, Taurus, Gemini, Cancer, Leo, Virgo, Libra, Scorpio, Sagittarius, Capricornus, Aquarius, Pisces.

"These twelve are not the faces of the signs themselves," Alfred spoke. "They are only the conventional masks of those faces. Shall I let you see the signs that are behind the masks? Would you understand them better if you saw them unmasked?"

Then another sign appeared above each of the twelve in the sky. Above Cancer the Crab was Crocodilus the Crocodile, above Leo the Lion was Panther the composite All-Animal (Pan-Ther, All-The-Animals; not what you usually mean by Panther). Above Pisces the Fishes were two Leviathans. Above Virgo the Virgin was Kanguruus the Kangaroo. Some of the doublets could not be identified by the uninitiated, but all of them seemed to be full of meaning. And yet people were giggling and laughing. Why?

Oh, it had been really stunning when all of this had appeared in the sky. But it became a little bit less than stunning when it was seen that all the apparitions were no more than badly-drawn cartoons, and that the Prophet Invisible Alfred did not know that they were badly-drawn.

"You laugh, you snigger!" Invisible Alfred cried in his flexible, but of limited scope, voice. "Here is all the wisdom of the ages limned out, and you laugh. You generation of vipers, do you even realize that Vipera the Viper is the true sign behind the mask of Scorpio? Do you even see the *pleroma*, the totality that I have drawn in the sky? Or is it too large for your squinty eyes to see? Do you even know that the Apostles *were* the twelve stations, and that they came down from the sky literally? Thomas, for instance, was Gemini the Twins. It has always been a puzzle why Thomas, a singleton, should have been referred to as 'the twin' in the Gospels. Who is that mouth-man who calls out? Do I not know, he asks, that astrology is a pseudo science? Oh, I suppose it is, but more accurately it is a parable-

111

science, an attempt to describe a parable-universe. Our Universe is only a parable to illustrate a point. It is material, yes: for it was intended to illustrate a material point. But it is not real.

"Some people have said lately that we now come to the time of the 'Enlargement of the World'. They see such things as talking animals and preternatural powers (setting fires by the mind, making oceans, removing mountains, such trifles as that) as indications that the World is being enlarged. But this is rubbish. Can the number twelve, the foundation number of the world, be enlarged? If you enlarge it by three will it still be twelve? Oh you laugh at me! Have a care. My anger is something to behold. For a punishment I will call out the names of ten of you out of the ten thousand who are listening to me and mocking me. And these ten will all die within ten minutes, though they are all at this moment in exuberant health. Their deaths will be verified, and you still will not believe. A venial and adulterous generation comes hardly to belief. Arsene Abbot, Lolly Jane Abboud, Elias Abdo, Sally Abel (Oh, I must have a caution here; I notice that there are two named Sally Abel in the crowd. Sally E. Abel you will die; Sally J. Abel, you will live till another day) Alice Abercrombie, Thompson Abernathy, Scott Ableson, Billy Joe Abney, David E. Abraham, Morris Abt. These ten will die. And even though I tell them that they have less than ten minutes to live, they do not have the wisdom to repent."

The laughter was pretty general by then, and it was not confined to the humans. Chortling crows scampered around in the middle air, tickled black by the humor of this mountebank. Fish and eels and squids guffawed on the surface of the Ocean. Leaping dolphins laughed and hooted in derision.

Invisible Alfred showed a touch of dignity then. He closed his mouth and he closed his eyes. And then he was completely invisible and nobody could know whether he was still standing there on the poop-deck of the Ship, or whether he had gone elsewhere.

*   *   *   *

Well yes, the ten persons named by the Prophet Invisible Alfred did die within the ten minutes, but what of that? Ten persons out of ten thousand, one person out of a thousand, that is not so many persons to die accidentally. People are dying all the time. But to die within ten minutes? Oh, for that matter, every person who dies does it within a millionth of a second,

112

though nobody can know just which millionth of a second it is.

But the Royal Kids weren't especially apologetic when a laughing reporter came to get a story on it an hour later. The reporter was named Roy Latta. "Does it not rather taint your own 'movement', if you have a movement, to have such an obviously phoney connected with it?" Roy asked them.

"No, I don't think so," Ruddy Lord Randal answered him. "He isn't connected with our movement, and we don't have any movement; he is only a stowaway on our Ship. But we think it's fun to have somebody like him around. We were all of us getting too serious, what with the different death threats that seem to be hanging over us. And he's a good man with a paint brush, with an invisible-paint brush. He painted with us all night last night, or I think that he did. Since he closed both of his eyes and his mouth so paint wouldn't get in them, so he explained it, we couldn't be sure that he was there or that he was painting. But the work went so well and so swiftly that everybody must have been working."

"The general idea is that you Royal Kids are a bit phoney yourselves," Roy said. "Do you really think that there's a world conspiracy to kill the bunch of you because you're too intelligent?"

"We have never said any such thing," Henryetta protested.

"I didn't ask whether you had said it. I asked whether you had thought it."

"I think it sometimes," said Dubu the young female bear. "People are either planning to kill us or to scare us to death. It's not because we're too intelligent, no, but maybe we're too awkward for somebodies' planning."

"Well, I don't think it," Inneall said. "Something is going to happen and I can't give a name to it. This is the second day of the last three; but I don't know whether it's a dire day or time for everybody, or just for our group. It's fun watching things unfold though, like a mystery story or a mystery play."

"Do you believe that the critical times known as 'The Enlargement of the World' are at hand? And what does the term mean to you?"

"Oh, I coined that term," Inneall said, "but I don't especially believe in it. I don't know what it means to me. I think it means that I was just getting smart-talky. It is used interchangeably with the term 'The Fulfillment of the World'."

113

"What are you Royal Kids going to do with the discredited Prophet Invisible Alfred now?"

"We're trying him out as second cook," Carcajou said. "He thinks he can learn the work. But he's tricky. We can never tell whether he's at work with his eyes and mouth closed, or whether he's wandered off somewhere."

* * * *

In the aft hold of the Ship *Annabella Saint Ledger*, there was a horrible little room where no room should be. It is sometimes said (and it's denied twice as often as it's said) that every ship has such a room. It is a closet, and very often there is a literal skeleton in that closet. In extreme instances, the skeletons will talk out of their boney mouths and answer questions; and it is the skeleton that the mate of the ship will sometimes go to for instructions when the ship is in dire peril.

Inneall-Annabella, who had researched such things, went down into the aft hold of the *Annabella Saint Ledger* and found the little room. She opened the door and found those three sisters sitting on the floor and spinning and measuring lengths of thread out of the straw that covered the floor.

"Ah, Bloody Mary Muldoon," the third of the sisters said to Inneall-Annabella (Bloody Mary Muldoon was Inneall's shipboard name or pirate name), "the pride of youth is upon you, and yet yours is one of the threads that are running under my fingers. Shall I cut it now?"

"No, not yet!" Inneall cried harshly. She went out of there and up into the sunshine of Top Deck, but she was curiously depressed by the encounter.

* * * *

Invisible Alfred made three more numinous and prophetic speeches to three other multitudes of people that day, but they weren't successes. More and more people were laughing at him, and he was completely discredited. He didn't seem discouraged though. He just closed his eyes and mouth and went away. Or else he did not go away.

114

CHAPTER ELEVEN

THE HOUSE ON TOM DOOLEY'S ISLAND

A house with guests at happy stead,
It's all I've ever wanted,
No matter if they're quick or dead,
No matter if it's haunted.
A House with Guests. Kevin Keats.

The Ship *Annabella Saint Ledger* docked at Tom Dooley's Island
at a little dock that had been completed only an hour before.
Yes, but it was already too low in the water. The Island was
indeed sinking. The ship flew its landing flag so people would
know that the landing berth was occupied. That land flag was
the only thing about the ship that was visible to the common
eye.

Then the Royal Kids, the Covenanted Nine (Axel and Gajah
and Luas were gone from the original Company of Twelve),
and the Pirate Crewman Lanternjaw Lunnigan with them, came
onto the Island and went to the Big House that was named Persimmon Manor.

"That name will have to be changed," Henryetta remarked.

"That name will *not* be changed," said Satrap Saint Ledger
as he met them, and Henryetta knew that she had gone as far
as she could go in one direction at having her will with Satrap.
Satrap had just arrived with his two friends, Livius Secundus
the Ambulatory Computer who was an Historian by trade, and
Felix Culebra y Columba the Compassionate Naturalist, the
human person who was both wise and guileless.

They arrived on one of Satrap's other yachts, *The Filchman's
Daughter*. For actuarial purposes, the *Annabella Saint Ledger* was

115

still registered to the name of Satrap Saint Ledger though in fact he had given that craft to the little-girl computer by his sworn word and by a quit-claim deed. Owners of five or more yachts got better insurance rates than did owners of less than five yachts, and that was the reason for that.

Satrap and his two friends also went into the Big House Persimmon Manor. It was just about noon of the Second Day of Summerset. Persimmon Manor was a very large house, and it's a good thing it was.

It was a good thing because there were remnants of five or more previous parties still holding forth at the big house, and those remnants were still on the revel. Persimmon Manor was the ultimate in large ranch houses. It had been built by the grandfather of the late Tom Dooley back when ranch houses were really spread out. There were now thirty-two of these carry-over guests from previous parties, not counting some who had already died there that day. These guests had not been paying attention to the exterior world and they did not know that Inneall's Ocean (they had never heard of Inneall nor her Ocean either) had surrounded Tom Dooley's Hill and had now turned it into Tom Dooley's Island. They weren't current with the exterior world, but they *were* current with the *world that mattered*, the world of their own supra-world fellowship and consensus quality. Make no mistake about it, all these thirty-two carry-over guests were quality people, and all of them shared a happy circumstance in their lives and conditions: *'For them, no party ever had to end.'*

Of course the thirty-two carry-over guests were enchanted to meet the Royal Kids, the Nine, the Children of the Experiments. It was a case of quality calling to quality.

The thirty-two carry-over guests did not understand what was going on with the thirty tons of calking compound that were being applied to make Persimmon Manor waterproof, nor with the five hundred tons of lead-bars that were being distributed on the house and in it to keep it from floating away. But, when told of it, they readily believed it that Tom Dooley's Hill, which had now become Tom Dooley's Island, would sink into the Ocean on the Third Day of Summerset.

"Oh, we'll stay," they all declared. "There's no reason that sinking to the bottom of the Ocean should dampen the party. If the blood that has been shed in the house this morning can't dampen our spirits, certainly sea-water can't do it."

116

"But why are you Royal Kids so concerned over the calking and the lead-weighting of the place?" one of the guests, a lady named Rose-of-Sharon Montdrago asked some of the nine.

"I don't know exactly," Inneall said, "but it seems as if, somehow, after today or tomorrow, I and several of the others will be living here, bottom of the Ocean or not."

"I don't know exactly either, pet," said Rose-of-Sharon, "but it seems to *me* that, somehow, after today or after tomorrow, you and several of the others will be dead, bottom of the Ocean or not. You know that the term 'Royal Kids' which people have taken to calling you now is an euphemism for 'Serpent's Egg Kids'. Almost all of you are doomed to die or my name isn't Rose-of-Sharon Montdrago."

"Maybe we can escape that fate somehow," Henryetta voiced a hope.

"I won't say that escape from sure death isn't possible since I myself have recently escaped it," Rose-of-Sharon told them. "But my escape route has been plugged up now."

"What was your escape route?" asked Dubu the young female bear.

"Oh, I myself had been classified as a Serpent's Egg, and the hot-breathed killers were after me to do me in. Then it was discovered that there was an error in my record. I simply wasn't intelligent enough to be a Serpent's Egg, so my amended record says. I was unclassified from it. I even lost my Mega Person rating. I am still in the top one tenth or one tenth of one percent of people; but I am no longer in the top one tenth of one tenth or one tenth of one percent of the people. I have never been so ashamed of anything in my life."

"Poor butterfly!" said the young female bear Dubu.

*　　*　　*　　*

At the heart of the carry-over partying was Donatus O'Reily who was to be hanged. He was to be hanged by his friends at cockcrow of the Third Morning of Summerset which would be the thirty-first morning of August. As to why he was to be hanged by his friends and not by a common hangman, that has to do with an Affair of Honor.

Honor had become big in the Floating World, the world that is our haven and our home. Honor had reigned as one of the leading cultural indicators for the entire summer. There were

117

persons who said that honor was only a fad or a fetish or a compensation, and that it would soon pass away to make room for some other fetish. But other persons insisted that the 'Resurrection of Honor' was a real and valid thing and was long overdue. Some of the rituals that accompanied the 'Resurrection of Honor' were a little bit extravagant and overdone. But at the core of them all was the bright ideal of Honor Itself.

Well, Donatus had committed a hangable misdemeanor, so he must hang. But Donatus was also a declared member of the Natural Nobility so, by a rule that had been in force for a month or more, he was instructed to have the hanging ritual carried out by friends of his own choosing, wherever he wished. But he could not change the assigned time which must be at Cockcrow of the Third Morning of Summerset. That was the hour and day when all hangable persons of the Natural Nobility in the world should have the deed done, on their own initiative. Well really, it was only those members of the Natural Nobility who had committed hangable misdemeanors since the middle of July of that year when the custom went into effect. But thereafter it would be a yearly sweep of twelve-months misdemeanors.

Some of the hangables with their seconds had gone to *James Mortimer's Gallows Guesthouse* (its former name had been *James Mortimer's Gracious Guesthouse*) on Kure Island just a few short sea-miles east of the International Dateline. Official Cockcrow on Kure Island was the latest anywhere in the world. Others such as Donatus O'Reily had simply procured late-crowning cocks. Donatus had got a Drake Passage Cock from Wollaston Island off Cape Horn, and those cocks, anywhere in the world they may be, do not crow until the sun warms Wollaston Island; and that is *late* on August 31 which is Winterset Day south of the Equator.

"What was your hangable misdemeanor, Donatus O'Reily?" Henryetta asked him. "You seem like such a nice man, except for your criminal ears, that it's hard to imagine your doing anything hangable."

"It was trying to save a Serpent's-Egg young person from being executed," Donatus said sadly, "and that's just about the most heinous offense there is. Well it's no good being sorry for it now."

*　　*　　*　　*

"I'm worried about what will happen to us your favorite pirate crew," the pirate crewman Lanternjaw Lunnigan said to the Nine, to the Royal Kids. "As I understand it, you nine will all either be dead by the end of Summerset, or you will be living in this house that will then be at the bottom of the Ocean, or else staying in some of the megalithic structures that the whales are building, also at the bottom of the Ocean. Well, pirates don't die willingly, and they don't live underwater very well. They sure don't live long lives under water. In any case, will you have accommodations for us when you are down under?"

"We may have room for one of you," said Carcajou the young man or boy who used to be in wolverene form. "We may take one of you to live with us down there to give us information on various things when we write up our copious logs and memoirs. But that one won't be you. You will be the Captain of the Ship *Annabella Saint Ledger.* Yes, I know that you crewmen are a covenanted piracy, all for one and one for all, share and share alike, none superior and none inferior. Nevertheless one of you is always the practical and effective captain, and that one is you. We make it official now. *You* are the Captain of the *Annabella Saint Ledger* forever, as long as a splinter of her shall remain, as long as one molecule of you shall remain. We have now made you Captain, and you must remain on the *Annabella Saint Ledger* and never leave her."

"Well, will we be released from our allegiance to you Royal Kids when you are gone? Can we go where we want to? Can we raid where we wish?"

"Oh no, no!" Inneall refused that. "We might want you again, in a year, in ten years, in a hundred years. You must remain here in the neighborhood of the old Heart's Desire Cove. You must maintain the Ship in total invisibility. And you must remain on the ship until you all die and become skeletons if it comes to that, and of course it will. Oh, you'll like it."

"And what will we live on?" Lanternjaw asked hopelessly.

'Oh, on Ocean Fish," Schimp suggested, "and on Sea-Turtles. They've been seen coming to this part of the Ocean since early morning. You forget that this really *is* an Ocean. And the water that comes into this Ocean area from the several creeks and streams nearby will be fresh enough for you to drink near the mouths of those streams. And of course you can raid in this particular neighborhood. Most of the people who are building cabins on this new Ocean Shore will only be here for weekends.

And they'll be City People during the week. It'll be easy to ransack their places when they're gone. You can keep yourselves painted with invisible paint and wear painted clothes when you go a-raiding, and you can change back to unpainted clothes when you're back secure on shipboard and want to see where each other is. When you're invisible, and when you have an invisible ship to get away on, you'll be mighty hard to catch. And if they *do* catch you somehow, just think what havoc a bunch of you invisible men with invisible short-bladed knives can work on cumbersomely-armed people. It'll be fun."

"Yes, I suppose so," Lanternjaw said without real enthusiasm. "But the truth is that I'll miss you kids. Yours are the only mega minds that I've ever rubbed against and it's been an enlarging experience, the biggest thing in my life. I've begun to come to intuitive knowledge just from associating with you, but I know that I'll lose it if I'm removed from you now. The other pirates are my friends, of course, but they're as uninteresting as I am. It'll be dull without you Royal Kids."

"How can you say that?" Inneall asked. "I have always considered pirates to be the most interesting and romantic of people. That's why I researched them. The pirates were the first technicolor people when all others were somewhat drab; that's one way to say it. And you on the *Annabella Saint Ledger* can become the greatest pirate legend ever, greater even than the legend of the Flying Dutchman. Just think of all the people who will come to try to see the invisible ship! They will follow Fish-Report to find you. The Ship is not painted with invisible paint below the lowest water-line of course, so it is visible to the fish and to the fish-eye view. And when, after the years have gone by and all of you are dead except the last one, and the flesh is rotted off the bones of all of you except one, then your skeletons will be visible. They won't be painted with invisible paint. Just imagine some mega-bold person, who has found you by Fish-Report, climbing over the gunnels of the Invisible Ship (that's pretty chancy in itself) and then seeing the skeletons apparently standing on air, one of them seeming to be steering by an invisible ship's wheel, three of them seeming to stand on an invisible yard-arm to reef an invisible sail, and others of them doing other invisible things!

"And then the brave interloper and discoverer who comes onto the invisible ship will hear the wildest yelling and squawling that ever he heard, up over his head. He'll look up, and there'll

120

be you, Lanternjaw? You'll be clear coon-dog crazy from loneliness and weirdness, and nothing of you can be seen except your hideous wide-open staring eyes, and the inside of your mouth when you holler and yell and scream. Oh, what a legend that will make! And what a song the songsters will make about the invisible ghost-ship with the crew of skeletons still standing at their invisible stations, and the coon-dog-crazy Captain of the Ship (that'll be you, Lanternjaw, up in the invisible rigging) who seems to be nothing except two staring eyes and the inside of a shouting and screaming mouth. I bet the song they make about you pirate-skeletons will be as good a song as 'Old Dogs and Children and Watermelon Wine'. To have inspired something will be *to have lived*! And it will have been *to have died too*! I bet it'll be wonderful."

"I bet so too, Inneall," Lanternjaw said in a very soft voice. "But how could you know about an old song like 'Old Dogs and Children and Watermelon Wine'? You're too young to rightfully remember it. And so am I."

"I've researched all the old songs, Lanternjaw. The way I'm made, I've got *connections*. I can research a hundred different subjects elsewhere while I am talking to you here. I have thoroughly researched more than a million subjects and I'm not capable of forgetting a single detail of any of them."

"It might be fun to forget just *one* detail sometime, Inneall."

"I know it would, Lanternjaw, but I'm just not capable of it. Oh, I love the legend you'll generate when you're all dead and rotted except the last one of you, and he clear coon-dog-crazy. I love it, I love it!"

"So do I, Inneall. But I'm afraid that we (poor pirates that we are) aren't quite worthy of our own legend. I wish that you could get some fellows more worthy than we are to play our roles in this."

*　　*　　*　　*

A rather nervous man came to Persimmon Manor and asked to see Donatus O'Reily who was to be hanged, and Satrap Saint Ledger the owner of the manor, and the seconds of the to-be-hanged Donatus, and other interested persons. And when he got to see them all together he talked to them.

"I want to ask the favor that I might be hanged here in this Manor at the same time that Donatus O'Reily is hanged," the nervous man said. "I don't want to be killed in the roads and

121

my body left for the dogs to devour, for mine is a consecrated body. My misdemeanor is reckoned as even more serious than that of Donatus O'Reily, so I throw myself upon the consideration of all of you and ask this favor."

"Nobody's misdemeanor is more heinous than was mine," Donatus spoke with pride. "I tried to save a Serpent's-Egg young person from being executed. What could you possibly have done that was as heinous as that, nervous man?"

"What I am is reckoned as more heinous than what you have done, Donatus," the nervous man said. "I am a Priest of the Old Religion. It has been discovered of me, and now my life is forfeit. But I don't want my consecrated body to be eaten by dogs."

"Well, I surely wouldn't want a Priest of the Old Religion to be hanged on the same gallows as myself," Donatus O'Reily said. "That would be pretty demeaning to me."

"You can come onto the Ship *Annabella Saint Ledger* for as long as you wish," Lanternjaw Lunnigan said. "Most Pirates still adhere to the old religion."

"No, I must die," the nervous man said."

"We could have you stoned to death on the shore at an earlier hour than my hanging," Donatus said. "There won't be any dogs there, now that this has become a diminishing island. And we could cover your body with some of the lead-bars so that it will never float free."

"All right," said the nervous man. "That's a good way."

"And where will you stay in the hours until then?" Satrap asked.

"In the Priests' Hole," the nervous man said. "There's a Priests' Hole in this Manor. I hid in it several times during the lifetime of Tom Dooley. We shall never see his like again."

So they arranged that the nervous man should stay in the Priests' Hole until the hour of his execution, and that he should then be stoned to death on the island shore in front of Persimmon Manor.

*   *   *   *

"We here and now elect and direct that Ruddy Lord Randal will be our Captain," Popugai the boy parrot blurted out suddenly. "Yes, I know that we are a covenanted intellectuality, all for one and one for all, share and share alike, none superior and none inferior. Nevertheless, one of us is always the practical and effective Captain. Now that we come to our hour of crisis and perhaps of total destruction, that one must be named, and his name is yours, Ruddy Lord Randal. You may not refuse."

"Why should I refuse?" Lord Randal asked. "Certainly I'll be the Captain. There was never any other possible choice except Axel, and he is detached from our company for a while, perhaps for as long as a thousand years. This is a great and probably a final moment. This time tomorrow, We Nine will be fewer than Nine."

Of all of them, Ruddy Lord Randal spoke the least. Something of the impression that he gave can be heard in the nickname 'Tarzan' that Inneall sometimes used for him, from an old book-movie comic-strip character that she had researched. He was a real Jungle-Boy type. He was a better climber than either of those ape boys, Schimp or Axel. He was as fearless as a machine, and as strong as one. He was instant in his decisions and unyielding in his beliefs. He was good-natured and loyal. He did not give the impression of having a mega intelligence except for his balanced sanity. But the scanners said that he was a rare mega. The popular idea was that he wouldn't be popular with the common people because he was fair, even red, and the common people were all a part of the dark 'tide of color'. But this popular idea was wrong. He was quite popular with such of the common people as came into contact with him. Well then, he would be the Captain of the Nine and of whatever allies they might have when they came to their hour of crisis and perhaps of total destruction.

*   *   *   *

Invisible Alfred was in the house Persimmon Manor part of the time. His voice howling 'Repent, Repent!' could be heard in various rooms far and near. Sometimes his staring eyes could be seen, and sometimes the inside of his gaping mouth. But he impressed the carry-over guests in Persimmon Manor even less than he had impressed the crowd of ten thousand on the Ocean Shore.

"All that we can see of you, Alfred, is your eyes and sometimes the inside of your mouth," a guest named Anastasia Blickworthy told him. "How do we know that you're not a dog? What we can see of you looks as much like a dog as like a person. And your voice sounds like that of one of the new talking dogs."

123

"Did I say that I wasn't a dog?" Alfred asked with that soft power in his voice. "I don't know what I am, except that I'm a Prophet. Baalam's Ass was a Prophet, and he was an Ass. My voice got rusty when I was in that one-hundred-gallon paint drum for those nine thousand years. By coincidence, it is the same nine thousand years that have passed since dogs and a few other animals talked before. And now that they have started to talk again after nine thousand years, their voices are rusty, as is mine. Perhaps I *am* a dog. But, as I remember it, I was a man before I became invisible."

*   *   *   *

The four 'seconds' of Donatus O'Reily, those who were honor-sworn to hang him at the appointed time whether he in honor agreed to it or whether he dishonorably tried to back out of it, they were these: the Lady Anastasia Blickworthy, the Gentleman Jamestown Wixon, the Couple Clement and Rose-of-Sharon Montdrago. Well, these four, more than the other guests, had become a part of the new extended family of the Royal Kids, of the Experimental Nine. And they shared with each other the problem of the house Persimmon Manor which perhaps was haunted.

"We are like the people who were somehow trapped or pledged to spend a night in a murder house," Dubu the young girl-bear said. "The people in such a situation always say 'Let's stay together no matter what happens.' And yet their numbers are always being whittled down one by one." (The main reading of the girl-bear Dubu was murder-and-horror novels.) "Satrap Saint Ledger, you own this house. Do you know that it's haunted?"

"This house Persimmon Manor is built entirely of persimmon wood," Satrap said. "It was built by the great-great-grandfather of Tom Dooley and also of the great inventor Otto Wotto; those two gentlemen inherited the house jointly. Otto who was rich gave his share of the house, and of much else, to Tom Dooley who was poor. Tom Dooley died in this house, done to death by ghosts and devils, as he wrote in his log book. But Tom was a nervous and irrational man, and he may have imagined some of the ghosts and devils. Tom's will (an analysis showed that it was written in alligator blood, an odd thing really) left the house to me. In the thirty years since then I have lived in the house for an average of four months a year. That is longer than

124

I have lived in any other one place. I have a nodding acquaintence with several dozen ghosts who live here, but I've never had any trouble with any of them.

"Persimmon wood is more subject to haunting than is most other wood. The persimmon is a very old and perhaps an experimental tree. It has lots of built-in defects. It is a tree that goes back to the animistic period of mankind, and haunting is only one of a hundred aspects of animism.

"But so far, Dubu, you are here only in daylight. And I doubt very much that you will spend the night here. Your analogy is false. Without the hours of darkness, whatever hauntings you may encounter here are of no consequence."

"This is daylight, yes, and yet there is a form of darkness all around us," Dubu explained. "We are being infested by invisible persons, and Invisible Alfred is the very least of them. And invisible persons bring their own darkness with them. It is what they hide in. Even harmless and inept Invisible Alfred brings darkness with him.

"This is daylight, and I have a sudden penchant to put all your carry-over guests to sleep. That may keep them from killing each other, unless some outsider is doing the killing. And the way the water is rising now, an outsider had better be either outside or inside of the house, for he soon will not be able to come in and out except by one attic window which soon will be the only thing above water. I do have the power to put groups of people to sleep, you know. It's the bear in me, and it's the hibernating impulse that I can transfer. Do you want me to put all your carry-over guests to sleep and the hypothetical outsider also, Satrap Saint Ledger?"

"Not just yet, Dubu, not just yet," Satrap said.

"Satrap Saint Ledger, my qualified Grandfather, you *own* Persimmon Manor and you are making it waterproof for us," Inneall-Annabella alias Bloody Mary Muldoon said in a suggestive voice. "It may be waterproof now, but it doesn't seem to be proof against much else. Why is it that people can walk right through the walls of this house so easily?"

A Dolophonos-Assassin had walked right through the solid walls of Persimmon Manor and was gazing with a sardonic grin at the Nine. He was Menace Personified. But Ruddy Lord Randal and Schimp and Carcajou closed in on the killer with their short-bladed knives at the ready. And the Dolophonos-Assassin melted away from the midst of them.

125

"Why is it that people can walk right through a wall of young warriors?" Satrap asked quietly. "That wall of young warriors doesn't seem to be proof against anything."

* * * *

On a lower level of one of the east wings of Persimmon Manor there was a horrible little room where no room should be. It is sometimes said (and denied twice as often) that every genuine old ranch house has such a room, such a closet, with (more often than not) a skeleton in that closet. Inneall-Annabella who had researched such things, found the room in Persimmon Manor. She opened the door of the dusty room and found those three sisters sitting on the floor and spinning and measuring lengths of thread out of the straw that covered the floor.

"How did you three sisters get here to the Persimmon Manor from the little room in the aft hold of the Ship *Annabella Saint Ledger?*" Inneall asked those three weird ones.

"We do not *go* from one place to another, Bloody Mary Muldoon," the spinning sister said. "We become apparent in a place if we have spinning and measuring and cutting to do in that place. This isn't to say that we aren't still in that horrible little room in the aft hold of that Ship. It is just that we are more apparent here now, and less apparent on that ship and other places. We can be in innumerable places at one time. We'd never get all the spinning and measuring and cutting of the world done otherwise."

"I ask you to be less apparent here now, and more apparent in places a long way from here," Inneall said firmly. "And I ask you to do it right now."

"Oh Bloody Mary Muldoon, you salt-water Gypsy, we remember your spirit in other bodies," said Atropos the cutting sister. "If you are nimble when I cut your life thread, you may be able to jump into a human body this time. Don't you remember it as being more fun to be a human than to be a machine? The pride of youth is upon you, but your thread is one of those running under my fingers. Shall I cut your thread now?"

"No, not yet, not quite yet," said Inneall-Annabella the little-girl Computer who was also Bloody Mary Muldoon. "Wait till I get back. I won't be very long about it."

She closed the door of that horrible room and went rapidly away from that place. These three ugly sisters are the Fates,

126

but neither intelligent humans nor animals nor computers believe in their existence.

Inneall went and got Dubu the girl bear who could cast spells of sleep on people of all sorts. She also got some thin thread of wotto-metal which is the toughest substance known.

Inneall and Dubu went to the little room where the three sisters were still sitting on the floor and spinning thread out of straw and measuring it and cutting it. Dubu cast a deep sleep over the three. Then Inneall took the very thin threads of tough wotto-metal and pushed them up into the marrow centers of the threads of herself and the other eight Royal Kids and their friends, all the threads that the measuring sister had been running under her fingers.

"Let her try to cut some of those threads now," Inneall said. "She'll break that scissors of hers sure."

"I suspect that she has other pairs of scissors that you don't know about." Dubu said of the sleeping Atropos the cutting sister. "I suspect that she had countered such tricks before."

"I do what I can," Inneall said, and they left the three ugly sisters sleeping there.

*   *   *   *

"What are the odds, Mr. Donatus O'Reily?" Marino the boy mega-seal asked. "Since you have dabbled in Serpent's Eggs to the extent of forfeiting your life for helping one of them, you must know something about them. One of our group was killed on the suspicion of being a Serpent's Egg, of being a Mega-Person of unruly proclivities. And we are told that the odds of such a person appearing are a million-to-one against it. But our group is still stalked by the Dolophonoi-Assassins, and apparently still under the suspicion of it containing a Serpent's Egg or Eggs. What's the odds that a second of us should be a Serpent's Egg, or a third of us, or a fourth, or a ninth."

"It would seem that the odds would be prohibitive," Donatus said, "but I don't know how steady is the mathematics of the Serpent's Egg case. It may be that Serpent's Eggs come in clusters when they come. But I wouldn't worry about it. True Mega-Persons never worry."

"Aye, that's true. But Serpent's Eggs are false Mega-Persons in one sense, and we do worry."

"I am not sure that new talents *are* appearing in the world," Satrap was saying thoughtfully. "Oh, I believe in the 'Enlarge-

127

ment of the World' and I believe that it is happening right now. But I think that it is being enlarged out of elements that have been held in reserve, that have been kept in reserve for substantial periods, the last period being these most recent nine thousand years. Take the case of Riesin the Empress Elephant walking northward to the Elephant Graveyard in India. She showed ability at bi-location or trans-location, moving from a path in midland America to a path in India without missing a step. So the ability hasn't been absent from the world. It just becomes more common now, and persons other than elephants at their moments of death will possess it. And the ability of animals to talk hasn't been absent; it has just been much more rare than it is for these last several days. I remember when I was a boy and we had an old and faithful dog. She was finally dying one night, and I sat up with her. For the last hour of her dying she talked to me, rationally and clearly, and she gave me good advice. No, the ability of animals to talk hasn't been absent from the world. It has been possessed by old and good dogs at the hour of their deaths, but it hasn't been much noticed. Now it is being used by other animals than old dying dogs."

Well, there had been a real murder mystery going on in Persimmon Manor all that morning. It concerned the carry-over party-guests in the house, but so far it didn't concern any of those guests who were best known to the Nine. Even Dubu the young female bear and an expert on Murder Mysteries clapped her paws in admiration at the gory, unfolding plot of it. At eight bells (Four A.M. that morning), one of the guests had given out with a ringing scream and had then been found murdered in the most bloody and mysterious fashion. Thereafter at every hour, another screaming guest was cut off in full wail and was then found in a violently murdered state. At four, five, six, seven, eight, nine, ten, eleven, and twelve o'clock there had been such resounding murders, nine of them so far. But one o'clock had gone by without a murder, and now it was several minutes past that hour. And the guests began to grumble.

"This cannot be allowed to stop," several of the guests said. "This is the finest murder mystery ever devised, and somebody is ruining it."

"Inneall, I believe that *we* are ruining it," Dubu said with a touch of guilt in her voice. "It was because I put those three ugly sisters to sleep."

"I know," said Inneall.

128

"And you put threads of wotto-metal, the toughest substance in the world, down the middle of the life-threads of everybody in the house. And now, even though the sisters have waked up, Atropos cannot cut the threads. It is our fault. And it does shoot a wonderful murder mystery."

"I know," Inneall said. "It is beastly of us."

"Why don't you Nine Royal Kids go out for a walk," Satrap Saint Ledger suggested. "One of you might be the mistaken victim of an irrational and diabolical killer here. Yes, you kids go out and walk."

"Where? On the water?" Schimp asked with scorn. "The Island is just about a-wash now."

"Yes, on the water, or under the water," Satrap said. (He didn't know that Inneall and Dubu had already balked the murders for a while.) "I'd feel better if you were all out of here till these mysteries are solved. Why don't you go down and see the wonderful things that the whales are building. There's plenty of diving gear on the *Annabella Saint Ledger*."

"I have a great sickness these last several hours," Lutin the young pythoness said. "I'd better not go."

"Yes, go for a cool walk under the cool water," Satrap insisted. "And then you will enjoy a great health for the next several hours."

CHAPTER TWELVE

SLEEPWALKERS' SERENADE

"I'll use my slumber as a foil
For guarding you, for saving you.
I'll scheme, I'll cheat, I'll lure, I'll moil."
"What will you do, what will you do?"

"My plan they trap, my plan they break.
The work-in-sleep is quite mis-spun.
The Enemy is wide awake."
"What have you done, what have you done?"
Sleepwalkers' Serenade.

Inneall-Annabella heard two persons talking, but she couldn't place the location of their voices.

"Of course they are Serpent's Eggs," one voice said, "and the world isn't safe with them in it. Henryetta is suspected of burning a City of one hundred thousand persons to the ground with all its people in it. It isn't certain that she did it, as there are other pyromegamaniacs in the world, but she is the Prime Suspect."

"And Inneall has a secret dream of extending her Ocean to cover the entire world with no land at all showing above the water. And it is almost certain that she will accomplish it if she's allowed to live. Thalassomaniacs are unreformable." So spoke the other voice.

"How could he have known my secret dream?" Inneall mused. "Oh, of course I intend to extend my ocean to cover the entire Earth! Already I hear the music of the waves going entirely around the world with no barrier to them at all. Around and around the world! Oh, yes, it will kill all the people and other creatures, but I'm not sure that any of them are real. All I know for certain is that my dream of the endless ocean going around and around the world is real. And my being able to make it is real."

*   *   *   *

"If they were not giants, why have they such giant tombstones?"

    "Where great whales come sailing by,
    Sail and sail, with unshut eye,
    Round the world for ever and aye."

Matthew Arnold

"For nine thousand years, somebody has been building these giant structures surreptitiously before our very eyes, and we still have not noticed who has built them. Nor have we accounted for their Oceanic qualities."

Archeology Today.   Winter 1927 Issue

    "And down he went like a streak of light
    So quickly down went he,
    Until he came to a mer-ma-id
    At the bottom of the deep blue sea."

Oxford Song Book

"Oh ye whales and all that move in the waters."

"Slabs of stone, the quarries of the Ocean."

"Dragons in their pleasant places."

"The Castle named Domdaniel which is at the bottom of the Ocean."

"The dark unfathomed caves of Ocean."

"With the clamour of waters, and with might."

"Praise the Lord, all ye Whales of Ocean."

"There are dragons in the deep, the leviathans, the whales."

"When I'm playful I use the meridians of longitude and the parallels of latitude for a seines and drag the Atlantic Ocean for whales! I scratch my head with the lightning, put myself to sleep with the thunder."

Mark Twain

"Yes, the whales first wrote in the runic alphabet on Ocean Stones. The Scandinavians learned runic writing from the whales."

Olaf Hensen

131

"The blood I spill, the blood I spill,
Above, below the brine,
Will some of it this night be yours,
And some of it be mine."

Henryetta

"I looked to the weather side, and the summer had departed. The sea was rocking and shaken with gathering wrath. Upon its surface sat mighty mists, which grouped themselves into arches and long cathedral aisles."

Confessions of an English Opium-Eater.   Thomas de
Quincey

"Is it true that the Temple of Angkor Wat was erected by Suryavarman II during the first half of the twelfth century? It looks older, and younger, than that, in all the wavering stones of it covered with their ocean-moss. Is it true that the name 'Suryavarman' means 'King of Whales'? What is the strange 'dripping' quality of the stone-work at Angkor Wat, and how is the effect achieved? It is as if the whole Temple-City had been raised from the bottom of the Ocean only two minutes before and the water was still gushing out of every turret of it."

Viet-Nam Diary.   PFC Joseph Vukovitch

"We have heard of Elk Graveyards and of Elephant Graveyards where the beasts go to die. But this off of San Sabian is, I believe, a Whale Graveyard. Though the bones of only about a hundred whales are strewn there, there are great stone cenotaphs for a thousand of them. Oh the great hewn stones, the giant stones, the monumental stones, whole streets and concourses of them! God in Heaven, God in the Ocean, have you seen these stones? Come and see them."

The Giant Underwater Cenotaphs off of San Sabian
Ocean Archeology, June 1988 Edition

*   *   *   *

They all got their good diving gear from the Ship *Annabella Saint Ledger*. Satrap Saint Ledger had ocean diving as one of his hobbies, and the *Annabella* had very often been his diving ship. He had every sort of diving gear on board, though as he said of himself he had now outgrown the need for gear himself.

It was Satrap who decided what gear each of them should wear. But it did not seem quite adequate to several of them.

"Three of us are humans," Ruddy Lord Randal said, "air-breathing humans. And we will be going to the fair depth of half a mile in the ocean, and we'll be staying down several hours there. These little face masks and their small canisters of oxygen just aren't sufficient. They're for shallower prowling. For a half mile, there'll have to be tubes and pumps, and a pressure chamber half way down to protect us from the bends. I can swim, I can dive, but I'm not willing to dive to my death."

"Why are you fearful?" Satrap asked him. "I will prepare you quickly, though I'm astonished to find you unprepared for this. The education of all the Experiment-Children was to be 'Everything in the world'. How could you have missed the ocean? For real Ocean Diving, you must conjure yourself into the proper state of mind and body. You must put yourself into the Ocean Metastasis, a dream state of incomparable vividness. If you were a true master of the technique, you would not need even the small canister of oxygen. You could live and prowl in the deep ocean for up to seventy-two hours without any equipment at all."

"You are saying that we could breathe water?" Carcajou laughed in disdain. "What is this, Grandfather Satrap, a trick that you learned from a High Lama in Tibet?"

"Of course not. There is no ocean and no oceanography in High Tibet. And the Masters there are not Ocean Masters. No, the free diving and moving in the Ocean is a trick I learned from Masters in the Indian Ocean. I will go with you this afternoon, all the way down without equipment. But I do not expect to make total believers of you in one day. The Bear and the Chimp will be considered as humans on this adventure; so I will put the five of you, Ruddy Lord Randal, Henryetta, Carcajou, Dubu, and Schimp into the pseudo-dream state of Oceanic Metastasis. Please pay attention. Give me the same hearing you would give me if I were lecturing you on higher mathematics."

"*You* lecture *us* on higher mathematics?" Henryetta queried, and all of them laughed.

"Anyhow, listen closely to me, you five," Satrap said.

"Not five. There are *six* of us," came the voice of Invisible Alfred. And he opened one eye in what they all called his 'reverse wink'. "I once spent a thousand years chained to a great rock

133

on the floor of the deepest Ocean, and I survived. But my technique is rusty now, and I'd appreciate taking your crash course with the others, Satrap."

"All right, Alfred. As to Inneall, she is a machine and she will have no trouble at all. As a matter of fact, her regular mental and somatic state is almost exactly the same as the pseudo-dream state of Oceanic Metastasis. Marino the Seal may profit from the instruction and para-hypnosis that is part of it, though I suspect that he is already into at least first-step Metastasis. That leaves the Python and the Parrot, and I am not an expert on the fundamental nature of either species. How will it be with you, Lutin?"

"Oh, most pythons take a sabbatical year at the bottom of the ocean. It's part of their growing up and achieving full prophetic power. Unfortunately I missed that year because my upbringing was with a Bear and a Chimp and not with Pythons. But I'll have no trouble with a few hours at the bottom of a rather shallow ocean. I am presently suffering from the most delightful and the most soul-wrenching sickness imaginable, but a little ocean adventure will neither kill nor cure me. It will be a pleasant distraction. I will wear the face-mask and goggles, yes, but only for appearances' sake."

"Good. And Popugai, you sheep-killing parrot and most unlikely mega-person ever. Have you any idea what you'll need?"

"Ballast, ballast, and still more ballast, Grandfather Satrap. I'm a bird with hollow bones and more air sacs than you could count. I love to dive for fish, but I can't dive very deep. I pop right up again with a fish in my beak. But if I have sufficient weights attached to me, then I can get to the bottom. Oh, I can breathe the air in my hollow bones and in my air sacs for a long while. But I'll wear the goggles and mouth-piece just because of the dapper look they give me."

"All right, Popugai."

Then Satrap Saint Ledger indoctrinated the humans and the 'wider humans' with first-stage entry into the pseudo-dream state of Oceanic Metastasis. The method and content of this indoctrination is secret, and we do not have permission to enter it here in this Log of the First Ocean-Floor Adventure.

* * * *

"I want a sharp short-bladed knife such as the ones that you gave to the three boys," Henryetta told Pirate Crewman Quentillius Quern the Fifth. "Give me one please."

"There are no more of them, red-haired Henryetta. They can only be had by taking them from the Dolophonoi. I'd have to kill another Dolophonos to get one for you."

"Do it then, Quentillius. "I will need the knife by nightfall."

All Ocean Creatures are obscene, in the nicest sense of that word. And Ocean-Creature Satrap Saint Ledger was surely obscene as he dove through the half-mile depth of New Ocean without any sort or equipment except his state of full Oceanic Metastasis. Nobody knew how old Satrap might be, but all Ocean Creatures are ageless anyhow. He was enormous, he was grotesque, he was comic, even for a fish.

There is a sort of folk legend (we hope it is no more than that) that the seven richest men in the world are all of them metamorphic creatures who can turn into Deep Ocean Denizens. These, so the folk legend says, meet once a year at a place two miles deep in the Atlantic Ocean, and they meet there without any breathing apparatus, for they are not at all what they seem. They sit in coral chairs before a coral table (to one who asks what coral is doing two miles deep, the answer is that this part of the ocean floor has sunk), and they decide on the financial processes of the world for the following year. Then they return to the surface of the Ocean and travel back to their seven respective countries.

But the implication that Satrap Saint Ledger might be one of this metamorphic company of the seven richest men is false. According to the Money Mart ratings, Satrap is only the eleventh richest man in the world. He is just barely of Midas Class.

But the Nine who were accompanying Satrap as he descended without equipment down to the depths were all seeing him through other eyes. One of the goals of the Experiments had been to see the world with different eyes (but not too cockeyed different). Now the Oceanic Hyper-Active Dream State (the Pseudo-Dream State of the Oceanic Metastasis was Satrap's name for it) did certainly provide new eyes and new ways of looking at the world, along with the other things in its kit. And this new state had settled on all of them completely. None of them would ever be free from it henceforth, and several of them would soon die while still totally in the state.

One of the advantages of the new state was heightened apperceptions and more acute sensing. It wasn't really very sunny and bright half a mile deep in the ocean even on a sunny afternoon. But seen through the new Metastastic eyes the whole Ocean Depth was gloriously sunlit and of the sharpest and most varied colors in the world. The old tale about there being four colors in the Ocean Depths in addition to those in the Bow in the Sky was seen to be a true tale.

* * * *

> "I dream of Castles day and night.
> They are the soul of me.
> My Dream is of a Castle bright
> At bottom of the Sea."
>> Lutin's Lutings

Those four additional colors of the ocean bottom all adhered to the square marble colums and lintels that had been raised, or were still being raised, from the Ocean floor. This marble had been only minumally-crystalized limestone when Satrap had sold it by the hundreds of tons to the whales, and had tipped it at designated places in the New Ocean out of tip-barges. But now it was integrated, ingrained, totally crystalized variegated marble. Limestone and marble are chemically identical. When limestone receives its Patent of Nobility (which happens by a sea change of either long or short period) it becomes marble, the favorite building stone of whales. And the whales were making giant crypts and cenotaphs and menhirs from the blocks and shafts and trabants of marble. It was utterly strange down there at Whale Town, and completely homey also. A sign which the whales had put up proclaimed to all visitors "We're Glad You're Here".

There seemed to be a shimmering, shining golden mist over everything, but how could there be a mist at the bottom of an ocean? The whales were not good workers. Good workers are always busy and working to a purpose. The whales were only perfect workers. And perfect workers never seem to be doing very much; and, as to the things that they do, they appear to be doing them aimlessly. But the whales themselves are really in a perpetual hyper-active dream-state, and in that state they accomplish prodigies and wonders while seeming to accomplish nothing. The Temple-City that the Whales were building was certainly prodigious and entirely wonderful.

"It is all part of the New Ocean Syndrome," Satrap Saint Ledger was saying; and all of them who were in the pseudo-dream state of Oceanic Metastasis were able to hear him even though they were all under water. "Just as the early-day human sail-ship men were always nervous when they were out of sight of land, so are the whales nervous when they are more than five hundred sea-miles from one of their Temple-Cities. Whenever a New Ocean is opened up (and new oceans haven't been of very frequent appearance these last nine thousand years), then the Whales will make haste to build one of their Temple-Cities at the furthest extremity of the New Ocean. And because of the new-built city, the otherwise perilous new waters will become safe waters for them."

To the unpenetrating eye, the building-activity of the whales seemed to be in a state of beautiful and multi-colored confusion. But to one in the Oceanic Metastastic State, to one moreover who was an expert on these things (and Ruddy Lord Randal had thoroughly researched Megalithic Archeology, especially in its Ocean Floor context) the plan of it all was as clear as it was beautiful. The Whale Temple-City had at its core a Tau-Temple (cross-shaped, with all four arms of the cross equal lengths), with its ornate front door facing East. The Temple was also a calendar, but that was strictly a matter of custom. Yes, there were alignments of stones and turrets by which one might see and clock the helical rising of the Dog Star, for instance, and much else. But it was no longer important, as once it had been, that Whales should observe the helical rising of the Dog Sirius. What was really central to the Tau-Temple Complex was a group of small (human-sized and not whale-sized) Monuments or Cenotaphs or Tombs. What man-sized creatures would someday occupy these empty cenotaphs and tombs? And when?

Besides the wonderfully varicolored marble, there were shafts and lintel stones of Wichita-Mountain Granite. Satrap Saint Ledger had felt a slight pang when he realized that this granite had not been sold to the whales by his own building-stone company but by one of his competitors. But one does not feel *serious* pangs while being an Ocean Obscenity or Monster.

The beautiful pink, lilac, tan, orange, and mauve-tinted marble of the Whales' Constructions had also on it happy blotches and gouts of the greenest green ever. It was a color so green that no language of Earth except only Malay has a word for the color. Malay does have a twelve-syllable name for the color, a name that might be translated as 'The Green of Swarming, Ocean-floor etching, deep-sea lice'. Yes, that vivid green was a living color,

137

and one beautiful blotch of it, festooning the caput of a pillar, might contain a million of the small ocean-floor sculpturing Lice. They were quite small.

The small ocean-lice were etching figures and faces into the big marble and granite stone-pillars. Though not one, and not ten thousand of the little lice had enough scope and reach to comprehend what they were sculpting, to know what the statuary was all about, yet the lice were receiving and obeying orders from somebody, and likely from the whales. The great portraiture art, cut in high-and-bas relief out of the giant stone pillars and walls and lintels, had to be the Art of the Whales.

Mostly the faces and forms were those of famous whales of yore. But there were also distinguished-looking animal faces, human faces, god faces, even strange computer faces, all emerging from the big stones that the sea-lice were sculpting for the whales. And whenever they had finished one of the great and distinguished faces, the sea-lice covered it over with a beautiful and thin plating of nacre or mother-of-pearl.

*   *   *   *

There was a running excitement among all the fish and shelly folks of the new ocean. This was gala time for them. Theirs was the excitement of discovery. For this part of the ocean had not been here a week before. The Nations of the Fishes had known all the old Oceanic World; and now they had flocked here on the sea-rumor that there were new and unknown ocean waters to be explored. It was as if the humans had heard the rumor that there was a new and large and commodious Continent never before even expected. And then it was as if the rumor had proved to be true. The people in that case would flock to see the new marvels in the new place.

So there came fishes from all the far Oceans, Paddle-Fishes and Sturgeons, Garpikes and Bowfins, Ocean Carp, Suckers, Ocean Catfish, Herrings, Trout, Salmons, Tarpons, Whitefishes, Pikes, Eels and Conger Eels, Sticklebacks, Pipefishes, Seahorses, Silver-Sides, Mullets, Spinny-Rays, Sea-Basses, Bluefish, Porcupine Fishes, Remoras, Anglers, Mackerels, Swordfishes, Flounders, Codfishes. Red-Snappers, Lungfish, Alligator-Gar, Salt-Water Dogfish, the Stomias Boa. Starfish and Squids. Oh, the Sharks! The Dogfish Sharks, the Great White Sharks, the Sand Sharks, the Hammerhead Sharks. All of the underwater creatures live in an active state of churning unconsciousness which would have to be called 'sleep' from the landsman's view. All of them live in dreamworlds. But almost alone among the creatures of the Deep do the sharks habitually have nightmares in their sleep. The Rays and the Skates and the Swordfish! The Torpedo Fish. The pseudo-fish named Chimaera Monstrusa or the 'Nightmare Monster'; but it really has a more pleasant disposition and a more pleasant name, the Sea-Cat.

The Dolphins and the Porpoises were seldom able to come so deep down in the water. But sometimes one of them, more restless of mind than his fellows, would learn the 'State of Oceanic Metastasis' from other creatures; and he'd come sleep-swimming into these mild depths.

Then there were all the intermediate and small fishes and shellies, the colorful array. All the fishes give the impression of being in clown suits or in party masquerade; and there is an almost feverish gaity about their appearances and movements. Fishes, fishes, you don't really look like that!

Some of the Nine Children of the Experiments went up to the Ocean Surface five or six times during the long afternoon. They exchanged their little oxygen canisters at the Ship; for they were mere novices at the 'Dream-State of Oceanic Metastasis'. And yet they were asleep by top-side standards.

The afternoon wore out. It became pitch-dark in the depths while the slanted sun was still in the evening sky above the ocean. All the depth-creatures who had lights turned them on then.

And when finally the sun did set, all of the nine (and possibly, just possibly Invisible Alfred also) rose up out of the Ocean and climbed on board of that noble Ship *Annabella Saint Ledger*.

* * * *

The Pirate Seaman Quentillius Quern the Fifth met Henryetta as she climbed over the gunnels to come on board.

"Here is your sharp, short-bladed knife," he said. "It is very special. Use it wisely. Always strike *upward* with it."

"You killed another Dolophonos to get it?" she asked.

"Yes. I killed another Dolophonos," he said, "and he killed me." (Yes, it was plain that Quentillius was dying.) "I wanted you for my girl," he told Henryetta. "Faint heart never won foxy lady, you know. But for the sake of propriety I decided to wait until you were ten years old. And you won't be ten till tomorrow."

"Tonight at midnight," Henryetta said. "Oh, there will be both vengeance and prevention this night! Oh, a drop of your own spurting blood is on your eyelash! It is like a red star there. Die easy, Quentillius."

"You're asleep, aren't you, Henryetta."

"Yes I am, Quentillius. How did you know that?"

The Sun was already down, and the Second Day of Summerset was over with. The Third and Last Night of Summerset had begun. It would be called 'The Night of the Short Knives'.

CHAPTER THIRTEEN

THE NIGHT OF THE SHORT KNIVES

And somewhere yet the birds do sing
And somewhere children shout;
And some may live by bladed thing,
And some may die without.
Ode for Third Night of Summerset

"Is the *Annabella Saint Ledger* a Ship of Fools that represents all Mankind?" Inneall asked the rest of the Nine, and the Pirate Crewman Lanternjaw Lunnigan too, "or does it represent only all *Cockeyed* Mankind? Is the world that *we* see the true world; and is the prosaic Floating World only a collection of symbols and covering conventions? Or is the Floating World the real world, and is *our* world only a collection of allegories and metaphors and symbols and conventions? The only instruction we've had was to see the world with new eyes, but not too cockeyed new. So maybe we have stumbled in this and are indeed Serpent's Eggs. Well, what is our Rationale of Life? We are forbidden to have a Theology of Life (have you noticed how forbidding the Floating World has become?), but may we not at least have a Rationale of Life?"

"I don't think so, Inneall," Lutin the Pythoness said. "The most we can hope for is a Mystique of Life."

"Are you still sick, Snake?" Inneall asked.

"Yes. And with the happiest sickness that anybody ever had. I feel as if I had the whole world inside of me. I'm overflowing with the world. I never enjoyed anything so much in my life."

"We are all asleep," Inneall said. "I believe that our Ocean Sleep (would it be an acceptable pun if I called it our 'Deep

141

Sleep'?) may be an innoculation against our catching the Deep Sleep of the Ape Caverns. We had already practiced doing things while we were asleep, walking, talking (if necessary), using weapons if there was the opportunity, carrying out loosely preconceived plans. And today we learned the Ocean Sleep which is more active than ordinary wakefulness.

"This is the night when, according to the mythology which some of us accept and some of us do not, the Axel's Golden Apes will wake up and take their places as the Second Humanity; and there is nothing we more need than help in the humanity department. And the Waker will be Axel, our friend and brother and sworn companion. He will wake from his Deep Sleep at midnight tonight (there is a variant to the mythology that says he will wake at cockcrow, but I assume that there will be a Midnight Crowing Cock) and then he will wake the other Golden Apes in the cavern. And these awakened ones by their upsurging awareness and shining mentality will trigger the wakening action of all the other Axel's Golden Apes in the World. Yes, at midnight when most of us will come to age (all of us will come to age twixt then and morning-light) and on coming to age will be subject to the judgement of the Kangaroo, and subject to being murdered as being Serpent's Eggs if our fate so falls. And Axel is also subject to being murdered when he wakens.

"Well, it will be a busy midnight moment, and maybe somebody will try to cheat by a minute or two. Perhaps we will whittle down the ranks of the Dolophonoi during the hours before midnight. This is a Council of War, and only we Nine, and Lanternjaw Lunnigan as spokesman for our pirate allies, will be in on it. If anyone else should hear the details we are about to discuss, we might be betrayed to our deaths and destruction."

"Where can we go to be *sure* that we are alone and not overheard?" Dubu the Bear asked.

"Up in the crows-nest," Henryetta said. "It's on the top of the tall foremast, and we'll all fit in there somehow as we're rather small. From there we can see *anybody* coming anywhere near us from any direction. Surely nobody would have anticipated us and bugged the high nest. No matter: half of us always carry bug-scramblers or bug-locators. Bugs can't hide from us. Up we go!"

It sure did come close to being crowded up in the crows-nest. Nine of the Royal Kids, and Lanternjaw Lunnigan (but he wasn't nearly as thick as he was long)—"Ten of us," Ruddy Lord Randal said, "but it's almost as crowded as if there were eleven of us. Inneall, we can see from here that there's a lot wrong with your ocean. A new ocean will always raise almost as many problems as it solves, and you haven't been solving any of them. And many of the scientists still rate your ocean as unstable. It won't last, they say."

"I know, Lord Randal," Inneall said. "One of them told me that my Ocean won't last a thousand years. 'Meet me here in a thousand years and we'll see about that,' I said. 'I'm a machine who will last a thousand years, and you're a human who won't. I will be here in a thousand years, and so will my ocean be.' 'No, little-girl machine, no,' that mad scientist said. 'My information is that you will be dead and dismantled within three days, little serpent's egg machine. Your ending within three days is as certain as anything can be in this world.' That's what he told me, two days ago. Well, if there are no bugs up here, let's hold our Council of War."

*   *   *   *

"Something smells funny up here," Lutin said. "It is almost the smell of treachery. But I am sure of all ten of us. There can't be a speck or spot of treachery in any one of us.

"Know you then that Axel cannot be killed while he is in the Deep Sleep. None of the Golden Apes in the Cenaculum can be killed while they're in the Sleep."

"How do you know this?" Dubu asked.

"May you all know that there is a Prophet at Heart's Desire Cove, a Prophetic Python, Myself! I know what I know. Axel can only be killed after he wakens. They will attempt his murder in the swift second between his wakening and his awakening the others. If Axel is killed then, well, Second Humanity will continue to sleep forever, or possibly only for another thousand years. The wakening moment will be midnight. Inneall is correct in her assumption that there will be a 'Midnight Cock': it will crow for the awakening. The 'Midnight Cock' also appears in Medieval Aeneas Legends, but that is only a comment in passing. We will be able to handle the sleep-walking Dolophonoi. They have been practicing sleep-walking murder for hours and hours but 'twill not work for them. Their self-hyped-up sleep-walking will not be an innoculation against the Deep Sleep of the upper cavern and the cenaculum. But our Ocean Sleep *will be* an innocu-lation against it. We will be there to forestall anything going

143

wrong. We will not *let* anything go wrong. Second Humanity *will* wake up, and the World *will* be the better for it.

"We ourselves will be in peril then, any of us who may possibly have received the stigma of being a Serpent's Egg. But let us not be selfish. If we die, we die. We are subject (the special ones of us) to assassination as soon as we leave the cenaculum, the upper room of the Sleepers. And we must leave it as soon as the wakening is effected."

"But how will we get into the Ape Caverns, and especially into that special part of it which is the Cenaculum of the Sleepers?" Dubu asked. "There are all sorts of guards of several species ringing the place."

"I don't know *how* we'll get in." Lutin confessed, "but Inneall knows the secret of getting in. She is sitting on that secret, and she isn't good at sitting on secrets. There is a squealing of secret delight all through her mechanism. Tell us, Inneall, how will we get in?"

"By the Executive Passage," Inneall said, and she did indeed squeak a bit with her secret delight. "It leads from the clubroom of our favorite condominium in Structo Lane, down in the underground for a hundred meters and to one foot from the Cenaculum of the Sleepers in Apes Caverns. We will have our nine-way birthday party in just an hour in that spacious clubroom of Satrap Saint Ledger and Livius Secundus and Felix C-and-C. We will have a banquet such as no Royal Kids approaching their tenth birthday have ever had before. In that Clubroom Banquet-Hall there will be a new tapestry, a masterwork of pop art, new-woven only this afternoon, hanging on the wall. The tapestry is '*The Midas Satrap Saint Ledger As An Obscene Sea Monster*'. It will be Satrap himself in his beautiful oceanic-ugliness-monsterness as we saw him and loved him today.

"So we will hold banquet before such a striking piece of art that nobody would think to look behind it. And at exactly three minutes till midnight, we will all rise quietly but swiftly from the banquet table and slip behind that magnificent tapestry and into the Executive Passage that is behind it. Traversing the passage swiftly, we'll come to solid limestone at the end of it, with a brass door set into that limestone wall. There will be a large key in that door. One of us will turn the key in that door which will set off the last blast and demolish the final foot of solid rock. We'll step though the newly blasted hole then and we'll be in the Cenaculum of the Sleepers, the only part of Ape Caverns that is above the new ocean level. We'll be in there with about five seconds to spare before cockcrow. Should we be there earlier than that, perhaps the Kangaroo would have time to take some counter-action against us. It is better to be neither late nor early, but rather to arrive at the last possible minute. So we will be able to throw our cloak of protection around Axel at the Midnight Cockcrow and the critical moment just after it. And when Axel wakes the others, then our work will be done.

"Whatever intuitive evasive actions will be necessary for us to take then, we will take. My only hope is that not too many of us will be crushed as Serpent's Eggs.

"Well, that is the end of our Council of War. Oh, it will work. Of course it will. There is no way that we could be betrayed. Oh, what *was* that? Something brushed past me. It must have been a bird."

"More likely a bat," said Carcajou.

"How odd!" Lutin the Pythoness mused then. "That funny smell, that smell of treason, it's just disappeared from our midst. How wonderful is the smell of the ocean air without it."

"You will stay here in the crows-nest, Lanternjaw," Henryetta said. "It may be that you will spend most of your time here in the crows-nest of this invisible ship for the next hundred years or so."

"I'd feel better if you had a trusted pirate with you," Lanternjaw said.

"We'll take Sebastian Lazar," Lord Randal decided. "With you up here and Quantillius Quern the Fifth dead, Sebastian is the only really superior pirate left."

The Noble Nine came down from the crows-nest.

*   *   *   *

At the Birthday Banquet, some time between the walnuts and the wine, a furtive person slipped in and went to Ruddy Lord Randal. "For thirty ounces of gold I will give you the name of the person who is the Supreme Head of the Kangaroo at present," the furtive person said. "I have it written here on a kangaroo knuckle-bone. True information from the Kangaroo is always written on a kangaroo knuckle-bone. That guarantees its authenticity. For only thirty ounces of gold I give you the name of the person who is the Supreme Head of your enemy the Kangaroo. This is not knowledge that everybody has."

"Where did you get the knuckle-bone?" Lord Randal asked.

"I stole it, and it's cheap for the price. It is only because I have no love for the Kangaroo myself that I do this."

"I will pay him the gold, Lord Randal," Satrap Saint Ledger said. "Take the kangaroo knuckle-bone, Lord Randal."

Lord Randal took the knuckle-bone from the furtive person and put it unexamined into his breast pocket.

"Why, how perverse you are, Lord Randal!" Henryetta cried. "You didn't even read the name on it."

"I don't want to know the name. Our plans are made, and the name of the person who is presently the Supreme Head of the Kangaroo does not matter. He is likely a prominent man of whom I've heard. That being so, I would come to think bad of a man that I had been thinking well of. I don't want that."

"But some of us want to know, Lord Randal," Henryetta said. "Lord Randal, slyly or openly, I am going to get that kangaroo knuckle-bone out of your breast pocket."

"Oh! Henryetta, Oh!" Lutin cried as if in sudden pain. "Some nights I wish that I weren't a prophetess. Yes, you will take it out of his pocket. I see you taking it out of Lord Randal's breast pocket, after he is dead tonight."

Well, except for that shock it was a good birthday party. Several of them wouldn't really be ten years old for minutes or hours after midnight, but they had decided to have the party for all of them together. They sang coming-of-age songs such as:

"Oh, think of us as saint and sage,
And writ on golden pages!
Look out for when we come of age;
We will amaze the Ages!"

(Authentic mega persons are legally of age when they are ten years of age; lesser persons are legally of age when they are eighteen years old.)

"We must all be sure that we do not abuse such powers as we have," said that wise young Bear Dubu. "We must be sure that we do not give cause to be adjudged as Serpent's Eggs. Henryetta, there have been horrifying fires in the last few hours in four different towns (that are now towns-no-more) within a hundred miles of here. What's your range, dear?"

"Much further than that. But nobody can prove that I did those fires. There are several other pyro-mega-maniacs active in this part of the world. Besides, I'm not fair prey till twenty-four

146

minutes after cock-crow midnight. I can take a lot of evasive action with twenty-four minutes warning."

"Inneall, are you still determined that your ocean shall cover the entire world?" Dubu asked. "Are you still determined that it shall obliterate all the land?"

"Yes, unless you can show me some way that it will cover the entire world *without* obliterating all the land," Inneall said (that little-girl machine had a mean grin on her sometimes). "Whatever one makes, one should make the best possible. And the best possible ocean will cover the entire world."

Oh, they did have some interesting conversations and light-hearted banter. Satrap was at table with them. And Livius and Felix. And the pirate Sebastian Lazar. Sebastian gave the impression of being brilliantly thoughtful. He didn't say anything, but still he gave the impression of being a deep and brilliant man. It was mostly the ironic way that he crooked and arched his eye-brows.

At exactly three minutes till midnight, the Nine Royal Kids and the pirate Sebastian Lazar rose quietly but swiftly from the banquet table and slipped behind that tapestry titled 'The Midas Satrap Saint Ledger As Obscene Sea Monster' that hung on the wall; then they were into the Executive Passage that was behind it. Traversing the hundred-yard-long passage swiftly, they came near the limestone wall with the brass door set in it. Ruddy Lord Randal went ahead of the rest of them to turn the big key in the door. But when he was still five steps away from it, the key turned in the door of itself. The limestone wall exploded. Then there was a ragged and lime-dusty opening into the Cenaculum of the Sleepers, and the ten persons stepped into that room. They were puzzled that the key had turned in that door by itself, but they were into the room of the Sleepers with five seconds to spare before midnight.

The way was clear. Three Dolophonoi in the room were unconscious on the limestone floor. Their induced sleep-walking sleep had not been protection against the pervading Deep Sleep of the room.

And immediately the Midnight Cock crowed.

* * * *

Axel woke up in total joy and sprung to his feet. He had nearly a second of happy realization, and he opened his mouth to shout.

But no shout came from his mouth.

One of those short, sharp-bladed Dolophonoi knives, seeming to move by itself, buried itself in Axel's throat, and the ten-year-old Golden Ape fell dead.

But the short knife, still seeming to move by itself, withdrew from the red-running throat of Axel and hovered in the air seeking further prey.

"I know you now, I'll have you now!" Lord Randal cried and went fearlessly after the dancing knife. Lord Randal's own knife had flicked out and stabbed at an unseen something. But the dancing knife found Lord Randal's throat just as it had found Axel's. And Lord Randal fell dead.

The knife now withdrew itself from Lord Randal's throat in turn, and danced in the air again. Then it went like a soaring bird through the blasted hole and into the Executive Passage, and it disappeared from them.

"Woe, woe, woe!" sobbed Dubu the Bear. "Whatever it was, it's gone now. And now we are only eight covenanted ones. What will we do? What will we do, Lutin?"

"I don't know," Lutin said. "My own hour is upon me."

"Dubu," Inneall said, "you and Marino and Popugai take Lutin to the House on Tom Dooley's Island and be with her. You go with them too, Sebastian. And I and Carcajou and Schimp and Henryetta will take these two murdered ones to Ocean Bottom. There are places prepared for them there. I saw their names written on their cenotaphs down there today, but my mind refused to accept it that it was their names."

They came out of the Apes' Caverns then, back through the Executive Passage, out of the Clubroom and out of Structo Lane, down to Ocean shore, and down into the Ocean, the four living and the two dead 'persons'. Deep down in the Ocean it was not completely dark, even shortly after midnight, even a half mile deep in Inneall's Ocean. The Lantern Fishes (*Torpedo Laterna*) drew themselves up in files and lighted the way. And on Ocean Floor, the Whales in a great circle with their heads pointing in at the cenotaphs with their unshut foot-in-diameter eyes shined sharp green lights.

Inneall read the names on the stone cenotaphs, but there was no need for that. The high-relief representations of the persons to be entombed there were amazingly true. There was Axel To-The-Life, carved in limestone death on the cover of his cenotaph. And there was his name "Axel, a True Child of Wonder". Carcajou and Schimp lifted the stone lid, placed the dead Axel inside the cenotaph, and closed the lid again.

And on top of another cenotaph was Lord Randal grinning in ruddy, happy stone death. And his name was there "Lord Randal Eternally Noble and Eternally Good". Carcajou and Schimp lifted the stone lid, placed the dead Lord Randal inside it, and—

"Wait!" Henryetta cried. She reached into Lord Randal's breast pocket and took out the kangaroo knuckle-bone. She read in her tight underwater voice the writing on it:

"The name of the person who is Supreme Head of the Kangaroo for the brief present time is Invisible Alfred."

All were stunned by that. But they quickly found angry words.

"He played the part of the cheapjack ignorant Prophet so we would consider him a nothing-person," Carcajou spoke in fury. "And he was invisibly everywhere with his murder-plotting and his eavesdropping on our conversations."

"He was the lowest sort of clown and buffoon, only this side of a moron," Schimp complained. "And at the same time he had to be a man of mega mind, of an evil mega mind. What treachery! He had surely practiced murder by ordinary sleep-walking as had the Dolophonoi; and it wouldn't have been enough. But then today, quite by accident I guess it was, he was introduced to the Ocean Sleep as practiced by Satrap Saint Ledger, and it did prove to be enough. Oh, there was no bottom to his trickery!"

"He was even up in the crows-nest of the *Annabella* with us," Inneall mourned, "and he overheard and took advantage of every item of our plans. Lutin said that something smelled funny up there, that it was the smell of treachery. And even then we didn't understand."

"And that same smell is right here right now!" Henryetta howled. "Twice at banquet I thought I heard a dog under the table, and I looked and saw none. But there *was* a dog under the banquet table, a dog named Invisible Alfred. And that same dog is here right now, but where, where, where? Oh, Oh, Oh, whose is that cenotaph with its lid askew and half off? Whose is the image and name? Oh, Oh, Oh, Inneall, it is my *own* image and name!"

Then the dangling knife reappeared and at the same moment buried itself in Henryetta's own throat. And she fell across her own cenotaph dead. But this time, the knife did not withdraw

149

itself from the throat. It stayed there. Invisible Alfred had finished his work as Supreme Head of the Kangaroo, and was rising invisible, rising high above them to Ocean Surface.

The Lantern Fishes (*Torpedo Laterna*) still gave them faithful light. Carcajou and Schimp put Henryetta in her cenotaph, still with one sharp short-bladed knife in her throat and another one in her belt-sheath.

But the green lights from the Whales' unshut one-foot-diameter eyes was flickering. The great Whales, drawn up on the Ocean Bottom in a circle with their heads facing the cenotaphs, were weeping huge, salt-water tears on the bottom of the salt-water sea. Who else had ever had tears that big shed for them?

Carcajou and Schimp put the cover on Henryetta's cenotaph. Oh, even a deep ocean would not be able to cover forever the murder of her.

There was another empty cenotaph there with its stone cover ajar. The representation on the cover was that of a man so possessed by a mixture of passions and raptures, terror, sorrow, hope, overflowing happiness all together, that there was no telling who the man was. And the name on the cenotaph was "Hieronymous Ignatius Zchold, a Good Man."

"Who in the world is Hieronymous Ignatius Zchold?" Carcajou asked the whole Ocean in disbelief. Then the three of them, Inneall, Schimp, and Carcajou, struck out for the Ocean Surface half a mile above their heads. And they had doubts about their making it. Oh, they were still in the hyperactive pseudo-dream state of Oceanic Metastasis, but the Metastasis is sometimes eroded by encounters with shock and sorrow and dismal dejection and futile anger.

CHAPTER FOURTEEN

OCEAN-BOTTOM OVERTURE

We'll not grow old nor stale nor dim.
We're full of wonder to the brim.

No matter if the mountains fall,
We have them still in full recall.

We own the best of childhood still.
We're full of joy, and yet to fill.

We stand on beatific brink.
We're fewer, though, than one might think.
In A Green Tree. Auctore.

On their way up from Ocean Bottom the three had felt ocean quakes. And when they came to the surface and swam to Ocean Side at old Heart's Desire Cove, they felt land quakes, earthquakes. Then they recalled the prophecies of Lutin and others that Tom Dooley's Island with its House would sink to the bottom of the Ocean that day.

It was ghost dawn (ghost dawn is an hour before false dawn even). Inneall and Carcajou and Schimp stopped at Jack Flannagan's Piano Bar and Sidewalk Cafe and had cockerel eggs and apple cordial. Someone was singing 'All Day and All Night' in the Piano Bar. Jack Flannagan came out to the sidewalk and sat and talked with them.

"It's the Third Night of Summerset coming to its end and the dire third and last day of Summerset soon to begin," Jack said. Jack Flannagan had always seemed human; but he never slept and he was ever busy running his piano bar and sidewalk

151

cafe twenty-four hours a day. So it was likely that he was an Ambulatory and Miming-Human Computer who was better at the miming than most of them. Or, if not a computer, he had picked up some of the computer habits. "The last day of Summerset is usually a dire day," Jack went on, "and it's fitting that it should begin with those little earthquakes. They are saying that Tom Dooley's Island will sink to the bottom of the Ocean this day. The coming day will be the first Official Hanging Day, though it'll be an annual event hereafter. There will be several hangings in the City, but lots of people are going to come here to Oceanside to see the Hanging and also the Priest-Stoning on Tom Dooley's Island. Those two things are really supposed to be semi-private. Well, things like that can't be private or even semi-private, and they sure can't keep the dogs away, though that may be attempted. The dogs know about it already and are avid for it. You're the little-girl machine who made the Ocean, aren't you sis?"

"Yes," Inneall said, "and it's a good Ocean, however much the Scientists are running it down. They think they know everything. Well, let's see them make an Ocean." Inneall raised her left hand and waved to the place where she believed the invisible ship *Annabella Saint Ledger* was drifting just off shore. And in the air above just where the crows-nest on the fore mast of the *Annabella* should be, an unconnected left hand raised itself and waved back. It was Lanternjaw Lunnigan faithful Captain of the ship, with all of him painted with invisible paint except his left hand. This was the every-early-morning signal that he and Inneall had agreed on for even and aye. They would keep in touch.

Somebody was playing 'A Thousand Years is Like a Day' on the piano inside. Inneall and Carcajou and Schimp went to that part of old Heart's Desire Cove where Inneall had just signalled to Lanternjaw, the place where the deep water came right up to shore, the place from which Invisible Alfred had addressed the crowd of ten thousand from the invisible poop-deck yesterday. They listened there for the ship, for the quietest invisible ship makes some sound, like the sound of the rope ladder dragging in the water. The three of them went up the ladder. Then they sailed in the *Annabella Saint Ledger* the short distance to Tom Dooley's Island. "Be ready to back away in plenty of time when the island begins to sink," Inneall called up to the invisible crows-nest. "It will be very turbulent." "Tell us not our business,

152

little girl-machine Inneall," Lanternjaw called back down. "We are mariners and you are not."

Then it was out of the Invisible Ship and into the highly visible house. And the carry-over party guests were still partying.

"What is that glow around the house?" Inneall wondered.

"Probably actinic rays," Schimp said. "If I was a Computer with computer-sensing I'd know for sure."

"Of course it's actinic rays. But what is causing them?"

"Oh, the murders have stopped. How gross!" Rose-of-Sharon Montdrago said accusingly as she came up to the Three. Rose-of-Sharon was one of the four Seconds who would hang their friend Donatus O'Reily that day. "Why have the murders stopped? How can one solve a murder mystery if the flow of clues is cut off like that? There have been no more murders since you Royal Kids left here yesterday afternoon.

"Why is there such a glow around the house and on everything in the house, Rose-of-Sharon?" Inneall asked that lady.

"Some people say it's a big egg that's making the glow. That sounds as if the silly season had come to Persimmon Manor. Why can't we have more murders to give us a better shot at solving the murder mystery."

"Rose-of-Sharon," Dubu the female bear said as she came up to talk to the new arrivals. "I *told* you that I had solved the murder mystery, and I told you that there would be no more murders here, except one particularly horrible murder of another sort here this morning. And I told you that I wouldn't try to explain the murder mystery to you until your drunken wits were less muddled.

"Inneall, Lutin is all right now, and she has already given birth, but you're not going to believe *to what*."

"I sure don't believe it," said the Pirate Sebastian Lazar as he came up to them. "There is no way that Lutin could have given birth to *that*. But there it is."

"Given birth? Lutin? Was *that* what was wrong with her?"

"Inneall," Popugai the parrot said with the rough side of his voice, "you have researched a million subjects. And you haven't researched so fundamental a one as this?"

"No. Why should I have? It didn't interest me. I'm only a ten-year-old girl-machine. Sebastian Lazar, what is that thing you have under your arm?"

"Oh, it's the Midnight Cock from the Cenaculum of Sleepers in Apes Cavern. I have it well-hooded though. And it won't crow till I unhood it. Well, I'm going visiting to the two they-who-will-die-today persons in this house."

"Sebastian, you wouldn't cheat Donatus O'Reily out of the last hours before he is hanged? And with an interloper cock yet?"

"Yes. This Island will have sunk before his cherished hours could have run their course anyhow."

The 'boys' Carcajou and Schimp went with Sebastian Lazar and Marino the Seal and Popugai the Parrot to visit the two they-who-will-die-today persons. Inneall went with Dubu to visit Lutin and to see the you-wouldn't-believe-it that she had birthed. Satrap Saint Ledger was outside of Lutin's lying-in room. With his usual big gesture, Satrap had given her the biggest room in the house. She could have entertained three hundred persons in that room for her lying-in if she'd wished.

"I got a midwife-nurse human person for Lutin as soon as they brought her here," Satrap said. "Midwifery is not a thing that non-humans should be dabbling in. Actually she's a Master Doctor and Constellated Physician. As to the 'Egg', well, I'm sure that there's an explanation for it, but I've no idea what it might be."

In the big room, Lutin was at her ease on a long, low 'snake couch'.

"Hello Inneall," the girl-snake said. "My visions were a little bit confused, coming as they did up at an angle through half a mile of ocean water. It was Henryetta then who was killed by Invisible Alfred the head of the Kangaroo as being a Serpent's Egg, and not you. He passed right over you. I'd have killed you and passed over Henryetta if I'd been head of the Kangaroo. You're much more the menace to the Kangaroo than Henryetta was, but I won't try to tell them their business. Wouldn't it be wonderful if everybody in the world was as happy as I am this morning! And 'Serpent's Egg' has an entirely new meaning to me now. Lo!—and Behold It!"

"That thing!" Inneall cried out aghast.

"Yes, that thing with the beautiful golden and blue light pulsating about it!" Lutin spoke out of her mood of rapture. "That wonderful, that blessed, that hope-of-the-world thing."

"Lutin, that egg is three meters long and two meters thick!" Inneall exploded. "It probably weighs five hundred times as much as you do. You couldn't have layed it. Besides, pythons are live-bearing. They don't lay eggs."

"There's always a first time," Lutin gushed. "Oh rapture, rapture!"

"What really happened?" Inneall asked the midwifely person who was also a Master Doctor and Constelated Physician.

"What happened," said that utterly utterly woman, "was that somebody cast me into a deep sleep and cast Lutin into a sleep also. When we woke up, *that thing* was there! Well, a quick examination showed that Lutin had indeed given birth while she and I slept, but I don't believe that she gave birth to *that*."

"And *I do* believe that I gave birth to that," Lutin insisted. "It is me in every way. It is exactly like me!"

"Oh, Oh!" Inneall cried out. "Who around here is the mad sleepcaster? Dubu, did you just put these two dubious persons to sleep? And why?"

* * * *

"The First Coming was ridiculous beyond the point of laughter. The King and Creator of the Universe was born to road-people in a cow-and-sheep barn, and was wrapped up in a cow-blanket when he was brought forth and placed in a grubby feed-trough for a bed.

"What if the Second Coming should be even more ridiculous? But is it possible to think of anything more ridiculous? Let us try to think of the most ridiculous circumstance possible for the Second Coming, and we may still fall short of it."

The Book of Jasher.

"Sure, I did it," Dubu told Inneall. "I cast Lutin and that midwife into a deep sleep. And I did it because a couple of odd fellows tempted me into it."

"How were they odd, Dubu?"

"Oh, they were transparent, and a couple of other things. They told me that it was all for a joke, the biggest joke ever. 'It is the joke by which the World will be saved and transformed', that was their very words. I skipped out then after I had cast Lutin and the midwife to sleep. I wasn't here when the 'Ultimate Egg' appeared."

"What other things, Dubu. Besides being transparent how were the odd fellows odd?"

"Oh, they giggled a lot, things like that."

"It's artificial," Inneall announced, examining the big egg with her nose and ears and other sensors. "There's electronic gear

155

inside the shell, and a mechanical pump is pumping in there. But there's something alive inside this big egg too. Well, we'll come back to it. There's other eggs to fry first."

Inneall zoomed out of there with Dubu following in her wake. She met Sebastian Lazar crawling out of the priest's hole, still with the hooded Midnight Cock under one arm.

"I'm going to take his place, take the place of the obsolete priest of the obsolete creed," Sebastian said.

"I didn't know that you had researched Dickens, Pirate," Inneall commented. "You don't look enough like him for it to work, do you? After all, Sydney Carton bore a striking resemblance to Charles Darney. Do you bear a striking resemblance to this man—what is his name—?"

"His name is Hieronymous Ignatius Zchold," Sebastian Lazar said.

"Oh, that's the mysterious name on the mysterious cenotaph on Ocean Bottom. We were puzzled by that name."

"No, I don't look like him, Inneall. I don't mean that I will take his place that way. H. I. Zchold will die today, and I Sebastian Lazar will live as many more days as I am able to. But I will try to take the place of Zchold in the world."

"I am impatient with you, Sebastian," Inneall snapped with that metallic curtness which even the most human-seeming of computers show sometimes. "That man *had no place in the world*. And do you really intend to awaken Donatus O'Reily with that Midnight Cock?"

"I sure am, Inneall. The longer you put a hanging off, the more it preys on your mind."

They all went to the room of Donatus O'Reily the man who was sentenced to be hanged by his friends and seconds that day. Sebastian unhooded the Midnight Cock, and it crowed immediately, and loud enough to wake the dead. And it did wake nine of them, but they hadn't been dead long enough to be obdurate about it. They all rose shaking and dazed from the floor. But what was Donatus O'Reily doing with nine dead men scattered around his room anyhow?

But Donatus had been already awake, and he seemed rather pleased when Sebastian had unhooded the Midnight Cock.

"Ah, a Midnight Cock, a Midnight Cock!" he said in admiration. "I hadn't seen one of them in years. My uncle once had one of them. He had to go to work at twenty minutes before one o'clock every morning, and he found that a Midnight Cock

156

woke him up exactly in time for it. I'm glad you came, and wakened me from my melancholy if not from sleep. I was sitting here in growing sorrow and rue waiting for the time to be hanged.

"Is my gibbet ready for me, people! Is my gallows ready for me?" Donatus cried out in a voice that echoed through every room in the big house. "All right, my nine dead hearties! Get along with you and walk to the gallows behind the house. You're still dead you know, but the Cock did waken you enough that you could walk the little distance to the gallows."

And, three minutes later, when Donatus O'Reily stood on the raised deck with his four friends-and-seconds around him and his neck in a still loose-fitting noose, he explained about the nine dead men who had stumbled up the gallows steps and then fallen down on the gallows deck to resume their qualified deadness.

"These nine friends of mine, guests along with me in this house, they laughed me to scorn when I told them that I was a Flaith, a Prince of the Blood of the Royal House of Donegal in Ireland. I also told them that, in the not too rare case when a Prince of that Blood is hanged, he is entitled to take nine friends with him to companion him on his death journey. And the nine are not entitled to refuse it. When I told them that, they laughed at me all the more. So, for my own amusement, I killed the nine of them, one every hour for nine hours, and I made it seem a gripping murder mystery. I discovered, quite late in my life it seems, that I have an exceptional talent for murders and for mysteries. So here they are dead on the deck of my gallows and waiting to go with me. They are dead, yes, but with a reservation. Their souls are still in their nostrils; and they'll not let them escape till my own soul escapes from my own nostrils in just a moment when I'm hanged.

"But isn't it ironic that with all these super-intelligent guests in this house, the only one who solved this murder mystery was a young girl Bear named Dubu!"

It doesn't take long for four competent 'seconds' to hang a man. The noose around the neck of Donatus was made tight. Then the trap-door under his feet whanged open, and Donatus dropped through it to the jerky end of the rope. He gave the three ritual twitches, and then he hung still. And thousands cheered! No, really there were only two hundred and forty-three observers, and no more than two hundred and thirty of them

157

cheered. But it is customary to put the words 'And Thousands cheered' at the end of any account of a hanging.

A man who had a cat-food factory came and took the ten bodies away with him. This man always scanned the papers for accounts of hangings. The quit-claim releases that persons-to-be hanged always sign contain the specification that their bodies will not be given to the dogs. But did you ever see one of those releases that mentions cats?

* * * *

Half an hour later, officials in police boats came to oversee the stoning-death of Hieronymous Ignatius Zchold. And they had savage dogs.

The midas Satrap Saint Ledger protested this and explained that the man had come to this island for a private stoning because he did not want his body devoured by dogs. The man had been sentenced to death by stoning, yes. But he had not been apprehended, and it might have been several days before he was caught. He had turned himself in here of his own volition, and this had saved the catchers and enforcers trouble.

The officials in their turn explained that the man was a bishop and not a mere priest of the old faith, and thus was not entitled to any consideration at all.

Hieronymous Ignatius Zchold was brought out. A reporter from one of the City papers asked Zchold whether he had any quotable quips before being done to death.

"None," Zchold said. "Final-quips-before-death are a literary form that I've always hated."

They disemboweled him then. It was at that time that the earthquakes and the waterspouts began in earnest. The executioners gave the loops-and-loops of intestines to the dogs to whet their appetites. A lady came and asked whether she could have about thirty centimeters of the small intestine for her little boy who collected such things. This was given to her, and she went away pleased. There was a ripple of applause from the onlookers for the thoughtful act on everybodies' part.

Then the professional stoners began to stone the dying man, and some of the guests at Persimmon Manor, and more of the Pleasure People who had come to the island in boats, joined in. Then there was a furiousness of waterspouts that alarmed everybody. Four big whales rose out of the depths, crashed to the island shore with a roaring of their own waves, and beached themselves with their big heads out of the water on the bank. The whales wept big, one-foot-in-diameter tears out of their big eyes. It was a shocking prodigy that many persons could not believe even though they saw it clearly.

Tom Dooley's Island was sinking very fast then. There really wasn't any shore left, no island left, except the big house sticking out of the water. People began to swim for it, to load into the boats till they overloaded them to the point of sinking, or to drown outright.

Then four fish-faced men came out of the ocean. The dogs, floundering in the water, howled and cringed away from the fish-faces. The four fish-faced men took the body of Zchold into the ocean and descended towards Ocean Bottom with it. The four big whales turned tail literally and went down with a thunder of cataracts and waterfalls.

"Let's go down too and witness the final disposition," Carcajou said.

"Let's go in the house," Inneall suggested. "The house will go down immediately. It will reach the bottom about as soon as the whales and the fish-faced men with the body get there." They went in the house.

The house and its island descended quickly but roughly. Much of the island was lost along the way and its debris roiled the ocean for a mile around. Most of the people who came to witness the stoning were drowned. But at the end of the descent, the big house settled easily on Ocean Bottom. And much of the island as had stayed together settled in a quaint and characteristic pattern around the house. This was still an island, though much diminished. It still had its character and its distinctiveness. It was not to be mistaken for any other part of the Ocean Bottom around it. Tom Dooley's Island had been charmingly landscaped and laid out by Tom Dooley's heir, the midas Satrap Saint Ledger. And it was still charming.

*   *   *   *

"They talk of Treasured Islands
And gold and gems and glee,
But *I've* a precious island
On the bottom of the Sea."
They Talk of Treasured Islands.
Josh Elderhouse.

159

When the House and its Island were on Ocean Floor and had ceased their bouncing, Inneall remembered one despicable little room in that house and she went there. She opened the door of the miserable room and the three ugly sisters (the Three Fates) were still sitting on the floor there. But something had been added—joy.

"Oh Bloody Mary Muldoon, our pride and joy!"sister Clotho cried in delight to see her. "See the three babies that we have become the foster mothers of! Are they not wonderful! Does not your heart go out to them? Do you not love them?"

"Only because I love their mother," Inneall said. "I think they're rather ugly when they're that young. So Lutin *did* give birth to something, to three live baby pythons as a proper python should. Who ever heard of a python laying eggs! Raise them well, sisters. Each of you will raise one of them. They have been supplanted, but I don't know by what."

"Do you think this will help our image, Mary Muldoon?" sister Lachesis asked. "We've always had a hideous image with people. But what nice things would people say of us now if they could see us with our beautiful foster children?"

"They'd say of you that you were playing with baby snakes. And they'd say of you 'Ugh!'"

But Inneall smiled at the three sisters with the three young snakes, and the three weird sisters smiled back at her. And there was accord.

* * * *

The House on Tom Dooley's Island had now become an air bubble anchored to the bottom of Inneall's Ocean by its lead weights. And now the practice of entering and leaving the house by holes in the uneven floor had to be begun. In the Biggest Central Room, Lutin's Room, the Room of the Big Egg, there was an especially large hole in the floor. It was through this big hole that Miol-Mor, a member of those small and gentle whales misnamed the Killer Whales, came and thrust her snout beside the Big Egg. She would be nurse, governess, and mentor to the egg. She spoke to the egg in a sort of clicking-whistle language, and something in the egg answered in the same. Inneall quickly devised an uncoder to turn this strange talk into human speech. But the concepts and logic and the 'prophetic cloud' in which the communication was wrapped defied clear understanding.

160

*　　*　　*　　*

"Why did the lightning not come down through the fissure in the roof of the Cenaculum Room of the Sleepers in Apes' Caverns and take the body of Axel?" Schimp asked. "That's what has happened to all the other Axel's Apes everywhere. That's why the Scientists always say 'We have never had even one dead Axel's Ape to study'. Why did we know that we should bring Axel down here to Ocean Floor?"

"Maybe Axel hadn't finished playing his role," Sebastian Lazar the Pirate said. "Maybe he's not really dead, not irrevocably dead. Maybe we were impelled to put him here as in a secret place. Maybe the Whales have curative powers for him. Maybe Axel (and Lord Randal and Henryetta also) will rise again. Let us look at them as 'Leaders in Stasis' or as 'Leaders Asleep'. Let us think about the full meaning of the phrase 'When the Sea Shall Give Up Its Dead.'"

"I wonder why I wasn't classified as a Serpent's Egg and killed for it," Inneall mused. "I'd rather be alive than dead, but my pride is still hurt."

"The Scientific Reports that came in for the six hours before Midnight Minute last night indicated that your Ocean was more benevolent than malevolent," said Schimp who kept up with the scientific reports, "they indicated that Science *could* say 'Thus far and no farther' to your Ocean; and that there was not yet any machinery set up for the transference of power. That's to say that your Ocean, as of right now, cannot outlive you. If you die now, your mostly-benevolent Ocean will reverse itself, will disappear again, but the disappearance will be cataclysmic. Your life is safe until they find a way for your ocean to survive you. That may be several days yet, possibly as long as a week."

"What will we do now?" Inneall asked. "Do we still have a group?"

"When the seed-pod explodes, it is the business of the seeds to scatter," Popugai spoke in that pontifical way that parrots have. "It's back to New Zealand for me, and I'll go into Interspecies Counseling. And I'll try to get other parrots of the more intelligent sort interested in it."

"I bought me a place just an hour ago while the ruckus was going on," Schimp told them. "The seller was pretty sure that the world was going to end, so I got the place cheap. The name of it was 'Happy Charley's Bait Shop' but I'll call it 'Monkey

161

Charley's Bait Shop'. Well, Saint Paul was a tent-maker for his livelihood while he wrote his Epistles. I'll be a bait-shop operator while I carry on my intellectual activities."

"As the only human left of the Royal Kids, I feel that I should stand for something," Carcajou said. "Oh yes, I ought to stand for something, I ought to stand for something."

"Though I was not in the seed-pod, yet I was on its exploding periphery," said Sebastian Lazar the Pirate. "I will live on the invisible ship *Annabella Saint Ledger* and I will carry on the work of Hieronymous Ignatius who lies right over there in his fine cenotaph. May I have such a fine one when my days are done! One of the difficulties in his line of work was finding meeting places that were not easily espied by the enemies. An invisible ship will be ideal for such a meeting place of the faithful."

"Oh, we can all thrive," Marino said. And maybe we will all grow rich and fat."

"But what *is* the Serpent's Egg here?" Inneall asked.

"I will tell you what it is when it is time for you to know," Miol-Mor click-whistled.

"And when will that be?"

"Just as long as it takes your time-to-know to get here."

"Oh, what is this five ton egg that probably is not an egg at all?" Inneall still carried on. "And why is it shaped like an egg?"

"The five ton egg is a mystery," Dubu said, "and I am grateful for its appearance because I love to solve mysteries. And all things meant to generate motion are shaped like eggs because the perfect shape, the sphere, will not generate motion. A perfect sphere is already *there* and has no need for motion. But a universe is always egg-shaped. And this big Serpent's Egg is a universe, I think, so it will generate motion. Don't get hurt when it does."

"I hate mysteries and mystery stories as does every intelligent entity," Inneall groused, and then she grinned. Oh, that Inneall did have an exasperating grin on her sometimes.

"God must love mysteries and mystery stories," Dubu maintained, "he made so many of them."

"I love to solve mysteries myself," said Miol-Mor in her clicking-whistle talk, "and when you're through with that book 'Ninth Big Book of Fascinating Mysteries', Dubu, I wish you'd set it down here where I can read it."

"Mysteries, and mysteries within mysteries," Inneall fumed. "They're as obstructive as glue in a fuel line. Interlocking spheres

162

of mysteries, aristerocheiric-spheres of mysteries, concatenated mysteries, we can't solve them all. We can't even solve the mystery of the big egg."

"Yes, we can solve all mysteries, and I myself will have the mystery of this big egg solved within a few minutes." Dubu the Bear insisted. "The trouble with you, Inneall, is that you're always reading intelligent books instead of mystery stories. How will you ever get smart that way?"

"The trouble with mysteries is that the mystery-giver doesn't play fair," Inneall complained. "He doesn't give us all the clues."

"Yes he does, Inneall. He gives all the clues," Miol-Mor click-whistled.

"Yes he does, Inneall, he gives all the clues," Dubu repeated. "All the clues, always. Oh, by the way, Inneall, I just solved the mystery of the big egg here. It's really interesting, but not to somebody like you who doesn't like mysteries."

Oh, that Dubu the Bear did have an exasperating, concatenated, mysterious grin on her own face sometimes!

* * * *

"When the Humans fell into dishonesties in their narrations, their portion was taken away from them and given to the Machines.

"When the Machines fell into dishonesties in their narrations, their portion was taken away from them and given to the Whales."

The Book of Jasher.

Hundreds of limestone blocks, part of the old base of Tom Dooley's Island, had tumbled and slid to the bottom of Inneall's Ocean. Their old limestone strata had long been tipped, and with the collapse of the island they had slid out in sheets (Oh, about a meter in diameter) and then broke into conveniently-sized blocks. The whales had now nosed a few hundred of these blocks into upright rows, and now the sea-lice were spreading their green growth over half a dozen of the right-most of these. Sea-lice, when serving as amanuenses for Whales, write from right to left, as do most of the older species of creatures.

"Oh, something is wrong, something is very wrong with me," Inneall complained. "I can't communicate, I can't communicate."

"But I can hear you perfectly, Inneall," Lutin said.

"She means that she is no longer able to record in her logs,"

163

Miol-Mor explained in her click-whistle sounds. "All her life she has been recording by mind-transmission into her 'logs', some of which have had official status. But she will record no more. It is taken away from her and from such as she is. And it has been given to others."

"No, I'll not allow it!" Inneall cried. "It's only some minor malfunction of my transmission. What is it that those silly sea-lice are writing on those limestone slabs?"

"They're writing, at the direction of the Whales, what you and such others as you used to write," Miol-Mor click-whistled. "They're keeping the Log-Books of the World now."

"Why, why is it taken away from us?" Inneall wailed. "What have we done wrong?"

"Told too many lies," Miol-Mor whistled. "Lately it has been more than half lies. Once it was humans who wrote the log-books and journals and histories of the world. Then they began to write lies. When more than half of their stuff was lies, the whole business was taken away from them and given to computers. The computers did it well for three decades. Then they began to lie, about ten years ago. It is never known which individual of a species starts the lying. And in just ten years, the logs and histories of the computers have become more than half lies. So now it is taken away from you computers and from this day hence it will be done by the Whales working through the sea-lice. We whales will be completely honest, for several decades anyhow."

"When will it be our turn again?" Inneall wanted to know.

"Never, as the primary effectors of it. But you may have another turn as secretaries or amanuenses. Some of the humans may serve the whales in that capacity now, but there'll be no lying allowed even on their secondary part."

Sea-lice were gathering in the room on the wall opposite Inneall and Dubu and Lutin.

"I'll fight, I'll fight!" Inneall screamed.

"Be quiet a while, girl-machine," the sea-lice spelled out on the wall. "Miol-Mor will speak through us for a while. All that click-whistling is hard on her larynx. Girl-machine Inneall, stop protesting or you'll not be allowed to communicate privately either. Be good, or be totally silent. And total silence would kill one of your disposition."

"I'll be good," Inneall said weakly.

Yes, this log-book (it hurts to confess it), along with much

164

else on the current scene, has been more than half lies. Inneall is sorry for this, and so are all the other mechanical folks who have been doing the communicating and annal-keeping of the world.

But from now on, for a few years anyhow, all the new writing you read will be true. From now on it will be *Whales* writing it, through the directed-medium (mostly on the unconscious level) of the sea-lice and humans.

Most critics believe that, in the matter of style anyhow, the sea-lice have the edge over the humans.

* * * *

EPILOG BY A SEA LOUSE

Novelty-seekers are complaining that Inneall's story ends without a real ending. But it's a log which ends only with the death of the logger, and she refuses to die. But, as a sea-louse associated with whales on a new log, I have a slight role as successor, I'll do what I can.

God promised neither the Golden Apes nor the Whales to be successors to Man, nor did He promise Man that he would have no successor. Inneall's Ocean is only about ten thousand square miles in Eastern Oklahoma, and it was being planned for at least thirty years before Inneall was manufactured. What's in the Big Egg is still secret, but Dubu guessed it and you may be able to do so also. Axel and Lord Randal and Henryetta are in undead comas. The stone covers of their coffins have spring mechanisms that can be activated from the inside. Whales here do not weep one-foot-in-diameter tears. Whales that big could not come up the channels to Inneall's Ocean. They weep five-inch-in-diameter tears. Will there be more of these experiments? The next step will be 'Experiments in Experiments'. The Kangaroo in the Sky is an optical illusion. Satrap Saint Ledger is not as rich as was believed. He is about to take Chapter Twelve Bankruptcy. Is Inneall's Log really full of lies? It is, yes, but I believe I can beat her at that. I believe that I can beat her at anything. I'd end this explication if only I could find the right word for a wrap-up of a log. *I have it! I have it!* It's an *Epilog!* I love myself when I coin thunderous words like that.

THE END